Dinah Maria Mulock Craik

A Brave Lady

Vol. III.

Dinah Maria Mulock Craik

A Brave Lady
Vol. III.

ISBN/EAN: 9783337111250

Printed in Europe, USA, Canada, Australia, Japan

Cover: Foto ©Andreas Hilbeck / pixelio.de

More available books at **www.hansebooks.com**

A BRAVE LADY.

BY

THE AUTHOR OF

"JOHN HALIFAX, GENTLEMAN,"

&c. &c.

"Be thou faithful unto death."

IN THREE VOLUMES.

VOL. III.

LONDON:
HURST AND BLACKETT, PUBLISHERS,
13, GREAT MARLBOROUGH STREET.
1870.

LONDON
PRINTED BY MACDONALD AND TUGWELL, BLENHEIM HOUSE,
BLENHEIM STREET, OXFORD STREET.

A BRAVE LADY.

CHAPTER XV.

IT was all settled at last, though after much delay, and very considerable expense. One fine morning the *Times* newspaper announced, in advertisement, to all the world that " the Rev. Edward Scanlan of Oldham Court meant thenceforward, in memory of his wife's father, the late Vicomte de Bougainville " (he inserted this paragraph himself, and Josephine first saw it in print when remonstrance was idle) " to assume, instead of his own, the name and arms of De Bougainville." These last he had already obtained with much trouble and cost, and affixed them upon every available article within and without the house, from letter-paper and carriage panels down to dinner-plates and hall chairs. His wife did not interfere : these were after all only outside things.

But when she saw, for the first time, her new-old name on the address of a letter, and had to sign once again, after this long interval of years, "Josephine de Bougainville," the same sudden constriction of heart seized her. It seemed as if her youth were returned again, but in a strange ghostly fashion, and with one vital difference between the old days and the new : then her future lay all in herself, all in this visible world ;—now—Did she, who had long ceased to think of herself and her own personal happiness, ever look forward to the world invisible ?

I have said Josephine was not exactly a religious woman. The circumstances of her married life had not been likely to make her such. But we cannot, at least some people cannot, live wholly without God in the world. Sometimes, in her long leisure hours among these old tombs, or still oftener in the lovely country around Oldham Court, where she wan-

dered at her will, feeling thankful that her lines
had fallen in pleasant places—the longing for
God, the seeking after Him, though in a blind
heathen sort of way, came into her heart, and
made it calmer and less desolate. Pure it always was, and the love of her children kept it
warm. But still it needed the great plough-
share of affliction—solemn sacred affliction,
coming direct from God, not man—to go over
it, so as to make the ground fit for late harvest,
all the richer and lovelier because it was so
late. As yet, under that composed manner of
hers, sedulously as she did her duties, complaining of nothing, and enjoying everything
as much as she could, for it seemed to her
absolutely a duty to enjoy, she was nevertheless conscious of the perpetual feeling of "a
stone in her heart." Not a fire, as once used to
be, an ever-smouldering sense of hot indignation, apprehension, or wrong; but a stone—a
cold dead weight that never went away.

Dr. Waters had given her two permanent
private advices respecting her husband: to

keep him from all agitation, and never to let
him be alone for many hours at a time. To
carry out this without his discovering it, or the
necessity for it, was the principal business of
her life; and a difficult task too, requiring all
her patience and all her ingenuity. Mr. Scanlan—I beg his pardon, Mr. de Bougainville—
was exceedingly well now; and with care,
might remain so for many years. Still the
solemn cloud hung over him; which he saw
not, and never must be allowed to see, or his'
weak nature would have succumbed at once.
But to his wife it was visible perpetually;
levelling alike all her pleasures and all her
pains; teaching her unlimited forbearance with
him, and yet a power of opposing him, when
his own good required it, which was almost
remorseless in its strength. As the wifely love
departed, the motherly pity, as of a woman
over a sick or foolish child, which she has to
guard with restrictions that almost look like
cruelty, and yet are its only safety, rose up in
that poor seared heart, which sometimes she

could hardly believe was the heart of the girl
Josephine de Bougainville. It would have
broken long ago, only it was a strong heart,
and it was that of the mother of six children.

She was sitting one day in the oriel window
of the drawing-room, writing to her boys at
school, when her husband rushed in and kissed
her in one of his bursts of demonstrative affection.

"Give you joy, give you joy, my lady!
You'll be my lady this time next week. I have
just heard from Lord Turberville. The address
is quite settled at last, and the deputation,
with myself at its head, starts to-morrow for
London."

"To-morrow! That is soon, but I daresay I
can manage to get ready," said Mrs. de Bougainville with a smile.

"You!" her husband replied, and his countenance fell at once; "my dear Josephine,
there is not the slightest necessity for *your*
going."

"But I should like to go. I want to be with

you; it is surely not an unnatural wish;" and then she stopped, with a horrid consciousness of hypocrisy. For she knew in her heart she would much rather have been left at home with her children. But, with Dr. Waters' warning ringing in her ears, there was no alternative. She must go with her husband; and once more she said this.

Mr. de Bougainville looked extremely disconcerted, but the wholesome awe he had of his wife and his real affection for her, though it was little deeper than that of the tame animal which licks the hand that feeds it and makes it physically comfortable, kept his arrogance within bounds.

"I am sure, my dear Josephine, nothing is more natural than for you to wish to be with me, and I should be very glad of your company. But you dislike London life so much, and I shall have a great deal to do and much high society to mix in, and you do not like high society. Really you had better stay at home."

"I cannot stay at home," she said, and putting aside all wounded feeling she looked up in his face, which happened to be particularly sickly that day, and saw only the creature she had charge of, whose whole well-being, moral and physical, depended upon her care. It was a total and melancholy reversal of the natural order of things between husband and wife; but Providence had made it so, and how could she gainsay it? She had only to bear it.

"Edward," she entreated—it was actual entreaty, so sharp was her necessity—"take me with you. I will be no burthen to you, and I do so want to go."

He made no resistance, it was too much trouble; but saying with a vexed air, "Well, do as you like, you always do," quitted the room at once.

Doing as she liked! I wonder how many years it was since Josephine had enjoyed that enviable privilege or luxury, if indeed to any human being it long continues to be either. As her husband slammed the door, she sighed, one long pent-up, forlorn, passionate sigh; then

rose, and set about her preparations for departure.

She left her eldest daughter a delighted
queen-regent at Oldham Court, with Bridget as
prime minister, promising to be home again as
soon as she could.

"And remember you'll come back 'my lady,'"
whispered Bridget, who, of course, knew everything. She had a dim impression that this and
all other worldly advantages had accrued solely
through the merits of her beloved mistress : and
was proud of them accordingly.

Her mistress made no answer. Possibly, she
thought that to be the wife of some honest,
poor man, who earned his bread by the labour
of his brains, or the sweat of his brow ; earned
it hardly but cheerfully ; denied himself, but
took tender protecting care of his wife and
children ; told the truth, paid his debts, and kept
his honour unblemished in the face of God and
man, was at least as happy a lot as that of Lady
de Bougainville.

The husband and wife started on their journey : actually their first journey together since their honeymoon! travelling *en prince*, with valet and maid and a goodly array of luggage, which greatly delighted Mr. de Bougainville. Especially when they had to pass through Ditchley, where he had never been since they left the place, nor had she. She wanted to stop at Priscilla Nunn's, but found the shop closed, the good woman having given up business and gone abroad.

"A good thing, too, and then people will forget her; and forget that you ever demeaned yourself by being a common sempstress. I wonder, Josephine, you were ever so silly to do such a thing."

"Do you?" said she, remembering something else which he little suspected she had been on the very brink of doing, which she was now thankful she had not done; that almost by miracle Providence had stood in her way and hindered her. Now, sweeping along in her carriage and pair, she recalled that forlorn, desperate, woman who had hurried through the dark streets one rainy night, to Priscilla Nunn's shop door, bent on a purpose, which she could not even now conscientiously say was a sinful purpose, though heaven had saved her from completing it.

As she looked down on the face by her side, which no prosperity could ever change into either a healthy or a happy face, Josephine said to herself for the twentieth time,

"Yes; I am glad I did not forsake him. I never will forsake him—my poor husband!"

Not my dear, my honoured—only my "poor" husband. But to such a woman this was enough.

Their journey might have been bright as the May morning itself, but there was always some crumpled rose-leaf in the daily couch of Mr. de Bougainville. This time it was the non-appearance of the Earl and the Countess of Turberville, with whom he said he had arranged to travel. True, he had never seen either of them, nor had his wife; the inhabitants of Turberville Hall and Oldham Court having merely exchanged calls, both missing one another, and there the acquaintance ended. Apparently, Mr. de Bougainville asserted, his lordship's delicacy prevented his coming too prominently forward in this affair at present, but when once the knighthood was bestowed it would be all right. And he was sure, from something Mr. Stoneleigh said, that the Earl wished to travel with him to London, starting from this station.

So he went about seeking him, or somebody like what he supposed an Earl to be, but in vain ; and at last had to drop suddenly into a carriage where were only a little old lady and gentleman, to whom, at first sight, he took a strong antipathy, as he often did to plain or shabbily-dressed persons. This couple had none of the shows of wealth about them, must, he thought, be quite common people : and he treated them accordingly.

It is a bad thing to fall in love at first sight with your fellow-passengers—in railway-carriages or elsewhere ; but to hate them at first sight is sometimes equally dangerous. Josephine tried vainly to soften matters, for she had always a tender side to elderly people, and this couple seemed very inoffensive, nay, rather pleasant people, the old lady having a shrewd, kind face, and the old gentleman very courteous manners. But Mr. de Bougainville was barely civil to them : and even made *sotto voce* remarks concerning them for a great part of the journey. Till, reaching the London terminus, he was utterly confounded by seeing the guard of the train—a Ditchley man—rush up to the carriage door with an officious " Let me help you, my lord," and a few minutes after, picking up a book the old lady had left behind her, he read on it the name of the Countess of Turber- ville.

Poor Mr. de Bougainville! Like one of those short-sighted mortals who walk with angels unawares, he had been travelling for the last three hours with the very persons whose acquaintance he most wished to cultivate, and had behaved himself in such a manner as, it was

plain to be seen, would not induce them to re-
ciprocate this feeling. No wonder the catastrophe quite upset him.

"If I had had the least idea who they were!
and it was very stupid of you, Josephine, not to
find out; you were talking to her ladyship for
ever so long. If I had only known it was his
lordship, I would have introduced myself at
once. At any rate I should have treated him
quite differently. How very unfortunate!"

"Very," said Mrs. de Bougainville, drily.

She said no more, for she was much tired,
and the noise of the London streets confused
her. They had taken a suite of apartments in
one of the most public and fashionable "family"
hotels—it had a homeless, dreary splendour,
and she disliked it much. But her husband
considered no other abode suitable for Sir Edward and Lady de Bougainville; which personages, in a few days, they became, and received the congratulations, not too disinterested,
of all the hotel servants, and even of the master
himself, who had learnt the circumstance, to-

gether with almost fabulous reports of the
wealth of Sir Edward in his own county.

Nevertheless, even the most important provincial magnate is a very small person in London.

Beyond the deputation which accompanied
him, Sir Edward had no visitors at all. He
knew nobody, and nobody knew him : that is,
nobody of any consequence. One or two of the
Summerhayes set hunted him out, but he turned
a cold shoulder to them ; they were not repu-
table acquaintances now. And as for his other
circle of ancient allies, though it was the season
of the May meetings, and he might easily have
found them out, he was so terribly afraid of reviving any memories of the poor Irish curate,
and of identifying himself again with the party
to which he had formerly belonged, that he got
out of their way as much as possible. *Honores
mutant mores*, it is said : they certainly change
opinions. That very peculiarity of the Low
Church—at least of its best and sincerest mem-
bers—which makes them take up and associate

with any one, rich or poor patrician or plebeian,
who shares their opinions—this noble characteristic, which has resulted in so much practical good,
and earned for them worthily their name of Evan-
gelicals, was in his changed circumstances the
very last thing palatable to the Reverend Sir
Edward de Bougainville.

So he ignored them all, and the "Reverend"
too, as much as he could; and turned his whole
aspirations to politics and the Earl of Turberville—to whom, haunting as he did the lobby
of the House of Commons, he was at last introduced, and from whom he obtained various slight condescensions, of which he boasted
much.

But the Countess never called; and day by day
the hope of the De Bougainvilles being introduced into high society through her means melted
into thin air. Long weary mornings in the hotel
drawing-room, thrown entirely upon each other,
as they had not been for years; dull afternoon
drives side by side round Hyde Park; dinner
spun out to the utmost limit of possible time,

and then perhaps a theatre or opera—for Sir
Edward had no objection to such mundane dis-
sipations now:—these made up the round of
the days.   But still he refused to leave London,
or, "bury himself," as he expressed it, at Oldham Court, and thought it very hard that his
wife should expect it.   One of the painful things
to her in this London visit was the indifference
her husband showed to her society, and his eagerness to escape from it : which fact is not difficult
to understand.   I, who knew her only in her
old age, can guess well enough how the petty
soul must have been encumbered, shamed, and
oppressed even to irritation by the greater one.
Many a woman has been blamed for being "too
good" for a bad husband ; too pure, too sternly
righteous ; but I for one am inclined to think
these allegations come from the meaner half of
the world.   Lady de Bougainville had a very
high standard of moral right, an intense pity
for those who fell from it, but an utter contempt
for those who pretended to it without practising
it.   And to such she was probably as obnoxious

as Abdiel to Lucifer. And so she became short-
ly to a set of people who, failing better society,
gathered round her husband, cultivating him in
coffee-rooms and theatres; new friends, new
flatterers, and those "old acquaintance" who always revive, like frozen snakes, in the summer
of prosperity, and begin winding about the unfortunate man of property with that oily affection which cynics have well termed "the grati-
tude for favours about to be received." These
Lady de Bougainville saw through at once; they
felt sure that she did, and hated her accordingly.
But have we not sacred warrant for the consolation, that it is sometimes rather a good thing
to be hated—by some people?

Longing, nay, thirsting for home, Josephine
implored her husband to take her back thither;
and he consented, not for this reason, but because their weekly expenses were so large as to
frighten him. For it was a curious thing, and
yet not contrary to human nature, that as he
grew rich he grew miserly. The money which,
when he had it not, he would have spent like

VOL. III.   C

water, now, when he had it, he often grudged,
especially in small expenditures and in outlays
for the sake of other people. His "stingy"
wife was, strange to say, now becoming much
more extravagant than he.

"Yes, we'll go home, or I shall be ruined.
People are all rogues and thieves, and the richer
they believe a man to be, the more they plunder
him." And he would have departed the very
next day, but for an unexpected hindrance.

Lady Turberville actually called! that is, they
found her card lying on the table, and with it
an invitation to a large assembly which she was
in the habit of giving once in the season; thereby paying off her own social and her husband's
political debts. It was a fortnight distant, and
Josephine would fain have declined, but her
husband looked horrified.

"Refuse! Refuse the Countess! What can
you be thinking of? Why, hers is just the set
in which we ought to move, where I am sure
to be properly appreciated. You too, my dear,
when people find out that you come of good

family; if you would only get over your country
ways, and learn to shine in society."

Josephine smiled, and there came again to her
lips the bitter warning, which she knew was
safe not to be comprehended, "Let sleeping
dogs lie." For lately, thrust against her will
into this busy, brilliant, strong, intellectual life
—such as everybody must see more or less in
London—there had arisen in her a dim, dormant
sense of what she was: a woman with eyes to
see, brains to judge, and a heart to comprehend
it. Also, what she might have been, and how
much she might have done, both of herself and
by means of her large fortune, if she had been
unmarried, or married to a different sort of man.
She felt dawning sometimes a wild womanly
ambition, or rather the foreshadowing of what
under other circumstances that ambition might
have been,—as passionate, as tender, as that
which she thought she perceived one night in
the eyes of a great statesman's wife listening to
her husband speaking in the House of Commons.

Even as she, Josephine de Bougainville, could have listened, she knew,—had heaven sent her such a man.

But these were wild wicked thoughts. She pressed them down, and turned her attention to other things, especially to the new fashionable costume in which her husband insisted she was to commence " shining in society."

When, on the momentous night, Sir Edward handed his wife, rather ostentatiously, through the knot of idlers in the hotel lobby, he declared with truth that she looked " beautiful." So she did, with the beauty which is independent of mere youth. She had made the best of her beauty, too, as, when nigh upon forty, every woman is bound to take extra pains in doing. In defiance of the court milliner, she had insisted upon veiling her faded neck and arms with rich lace, and giving stateliness to her tall thin figure by sweeping folds of black velvet. Also, instead of foolish artificial flowers in her grey hair, she wore a sort of head-dress, simple yet regal, which made her look, as her maid declared, " like a picture." She did not try to be young: she could not help being beautiful.

Enchanted with her appearance, her husband called her exuberantly "his jewel;" which no doubt she was; only he had no wish, like the tender Scotch lover, to "wear her in his bosom" —he would much have preferred to plant her in his cap-front, in a gorgeous setting, for all the world to gaze at. Her value to him was not what she was in herself, but what she appeared to other people.

Therefore, when he saw her contrasted with the brillant crowd which straggled up the staircase of Turberville House, his enthusiastic admiration of her a little cooled down.

"How dark you look in that black gown! There's something not right about you, not like these other ladies. I see what it is, you dress yourself in far too old-fashioned and too plain a style. Very provoking! when I wanted you to appear your best before her ladyship."

"She will never see me in this crowd," was all Josephine answered, or had time to answer,

being drifted apart from her husband, who dart-
ed after a face he thought he knew.

In the pause, while, half amused, half bewildered, she looked on at this her first specimen
of what Sir Edward called "society," Lady de
Bougainville heard accidentally a few comments
on Sir Edward from two young men, who apparently recognised him, but, naturally, not
her.

"That man is a fool—a perfect fool. And
such a conceited fool too!—you should hear
him in the lobby of the House, chattering about
his friend the Earl, to whom he thinks himself
of such importance. Who is he, do you know?"

"Oh, a country squire, just knighted. Not a
bad fellow, I believe, very rich, and with such a
charming wife! Might do well enough among
his familiar turnips, but here! Why will he make
himself such an ass?"

To be half conscious of a truth one's self, and
to hear it broadly stated by other people, are
two very different things. Josephine shrank
back, feeling for the moment as if whipped with

nettles; till she remembered they were only
nettles, not swords. No moral delinquency had
been cast up against her husband; and for the
rest, what did it matter?—she knew it all before; and, in spite of her fine French sense of
comme il faut, and her pure high breeding, she
had learnt to put up with it. She could do so
still.

Pushing with difficulty through the throng,
she rejoined Sir Edward. " Keep close to me,"
she said. " Don't leave me again, pray."

" Very well, my dear; but—Ah ! there are two
friends of mine !"

And in his impulsive way he introduced to her
at once the very young men who had been
speaking of him.

Lady de Bougainville bowed, looking them
both right in the face with those stern, unflinching
eyes of hers ; and, young men of fashion as they
were, they both blushed scarlet. Then, putting
her arm through her husband's, she walked deliberately on, carrying her head very erect, to
the select circle where, glittering under a blaze

of ancestral diamonds, and scarcely recognisable as the old lady who had travelled in such quiet, almost shabby simplicity, stood the little, brown, withered, but still courtly and dignified Countess of Turberville.

"Stop," whispered Sir Edward, in unwonted timidity. "It is so very—very awkward. I do hope her ladyship has forgotten. Must I apologise? What in the world am I to say to her! Josephine, do stop one minute."

Josephine obeyed.

And here let me too pause, lest I might be misconstrued in the picture which I draw—I own in not too flattering colours—of Sir Edward de Bougainville.

It was not his low origin, not the shadow of the Scanlan porter-bottles, which made him what he was. I have known gentlemen whose fathers were ploughmen—nay, the truest gentleman I ever knew was the son of a working mechanic. And I have seen boors, who had titles, and who, in spite of the noble lineage of centuries, were boors still. What made this man vulgar was the innate coarseness of his nature, lacquered over with superficial refinement. He was, in fact, that which, in all ranks of life, is the very opposite of a gentleman—a sham. I do not love him, but I will not be unfair to him; and if I hold him up to contempt, I wish it clearly to be understood what are the things I despise him for.

Did his wife despise him? How can one tell? We often meet men and their wives, concerning whom we ask of ourselves the same question, and wonder how they ever came to be united; yet the wives move in society with smiling countenances, and perform unshrinkingly their various duties, as Lady de Bougainville performed hers.

"Shall we go on now?" she said, and led her husband forward to the dreadful ordeal.

But it passed over quite harmlessly—rather worse than harmlessly; for the Countess merely bowed, smiling upon them as upon all her other guests, and apparently scarcely recognising them, in that dense, ever-moving throng.

They went on with it, and never saw their hostess again all the evening. The sole reward they gained for three hours of pushing and scrambling, heated rooms, and an infinitesimal quantity of refreshment, was the pleasure of seeing their names in the paper next day among the Countess of Turberville's four hundred invited guests.

This was Lady de Bougainville's first and last experience of " shining in society "—that is, London society, which alone Sir Edward thought worth anything. He paid for it with several days of illness, brought on by the heat and excitement, and perhaps the disappointment too, though to the latter he never owned. After that he was glad to go home.

Oh ! how Josephine's heart leaped when she saw, nestling among the green hills, the grey outline of Oldham Court ! She had, more than any one I ever knew, the quality of adhesiveness, not only to persons but places. She had loved Wren's Nest, though her husband's incessant schemes for quitting it, and her own con-

stant terror for the future, made her never feel
settled there; but Oldham Court, besides being
her ideal of a house to live in, was her own
house, her home, from which fate now seemed
powerless to uproot her. She clung to it, as,
had she been one of those happy wives who
carry their home about with them, she never
might have clung; but things being as they
were, it was well she did do so—well that she
could accept what she had, and rejoice in it,
without craving for the impossible.

After their return, she had a wonderfully
quiet and happy summer. Her children came
about her, from school and college, enjoying
their holidays the more for the hard work between. And her husband found something to
do, something to amuse himself with; he was
appointed a magistrate for the county, and devoted himself, with all his Irish eagerness after
novelty, to the administration of justice upon
all offenders. Being not only a magistrate but
a clergyman, he considered himself bound to lay
on the moral whip as heavily as possible, until

his wife, who had long lost with him the title of " Themis," sometimes found it necessary to go after him, not as Justice, but as Mercy, binding up the wounds he made.

" You see," he said, " in my position, and with the morality of the whole district in my keeping, I must be severe.   I must pass over nothing, or people will think I am lax myself."

And many was the poor fellow he committed to the county gaol for having unfortunately a fish in his hat, or a young leveret in his pocket; many was the case of petty larceny that he dealt with according to the utmost rigour of the law.   It was his chief amusement, this rigid exercise of authority, and he really enjoyed it exceedingly.

Happily, it served to take off his attention from his three sons, who were coming to that age, when to press the yoke of paternal rule too tightly upon young growing shoulders is sometimes rather dangerous.   All the boys, César especially, instinctively gave their father as wide a berth as possible.   Not that he ignored them as he once used to do ; on the contrary, to strangers he was very fond of talking about " my eldest son at Oxford," and " my two boys who are just going to Rugby." But inside the house he interfered little with them, and had no more of their company than was inevitable.

With their mother it was quite different. Now, as heretofore, she was all in all to them, and they to her. Walking, riding, or driving together, they had her quite to themselves : enjoying with her the new-found luxuries of their life.

" Mamma, how beautiful you look in that nice gown !—the very picture of a Lady de Bougainville !" they would say, in their fond boyish admiration. And she, when she watched them ride out on their pretty ponies, and was able to give them dogs and guns, and every thing that boys delight in, exulted in the fortunate wealth, and blessed Mr. Oldham in her heart.

In truth, under the strong maternal influence, and almost wholly maternal guidance, her sons were growing up everything that she desired to see them. Making all allowance for the tender exaggerations of memory—I believe, even from Bridget's account, that the young De Bougainvilles must have been very good boys —honest, candid, generous, affectionate; the comfort and pride of their happy mother during their first year of prosperity.

Even after she had despatched them, each by turn, to school and college, she was not sad. She had only sent them away to do their fitting work in the world, and she knew they would do it well. She trusted them, young as they were, and oh! the blessing of trust!—almost greater than that of love. And she had plenty of love, too, daily surrounding her, both from the boys away and the three girls at home.

With one or other of her six children her time and thoughts were incessantly occupied. Mothers, real mothers, be they rich or poor, have seldom leisure either to grow morbid or to grieve.

Of all the many portraits extant of her, perhaps the one I like the best is a daguerreotype by Claudet, this taken during the bright year. It is not a flattered likeness, of course—the grey hairs and wrinkles are plain to be seen—but it has a sweetness, a composed, placid content, greater than any other of the various portraits of Lady de Bougainville.

It came home from London, she once told me, on a very momentous day, so much so that it was put aside, locked up, and never looked at for months and years.

Some hours before, she had parted from her eldest boy, who was returning to Oxford, sorry to leave his mother and his home, but yet glad to be at work again. She had sent him off, driving his father, who had to take his place for the first time on the bench of magistrates, to the county town, and now sat thinking of her son —how exactly he looked the character of "the young heir," and how excessively like he was to her own father—outwardly and inwardly every inch a De Bougainville. He seemed to grow up

day by day in her sight, as Wordsworth's
Young Romilly in that of his mother, "a delightful tree"—

"And proudly did his branches wave."

She felt that under their shadow she might yet
rejoice, and have in her declining age many
blessed days.   Days as calm and lovely as this
October afternoon ; when the hills lay quiet,
transfigured in golden light, and the old grey
house itself shone with a beauty as sweet and
yet solemn as that of an old woman's face : the
face that sometimes, when she looked in the
glass, she tried to fancy, wondering how her sons
would look at it some of these days.   Only
her sons.   For the world outside, and its comments upon her, Josephine, from first to last,
never cared two straws.

Yet she was not unsocial, and sometimes,
both for herself and her children's sake, would
have preferred a less lonely life than they had
at Oldham Court—would have liked occasionally to mix with persons of her own sphere and
on the level of her own cultivation.   Now her

only friends were the poor people of the neighbourhood, among whom she went about a good
deal, and who looked up to her as to the Lady
Bountiful of the whole country-side.

But that day she had enjoyed some pleasure
in a long talk with the last person she expected
to see or to fraternise with—Lady Turberville.
They had met at the cottage of an old woman
to whom Josephine had been very kind. The
Countess also; only, as she herself owned, her
charities were necessarily limited. " You are
a much richer woman than I," she had said, with
a proud frankness, as she stood tucking up her
gown-skirt to walk back the three miles to the
Hall, and eyed with good-natured, but half satirical glance, Lady de Bougainville's splendid
carriage, which had just drawn up to the cot-
tage-door.

Josephine explained that she had intended
to take the paralytic old woman for a drive.

"But since it rains so fast, if Lady Turberville would——"

" If she would give you the chance of being

kind to one old woman instead of another?
Well, as I am rheumatic, and neighbourly kindness is pleasant, will you drive me home?"

"Gladly," said Lady de Bougainville. And
they became quite friendly before they reached
the Hall.

Altogether the strong shrewd simplicity of
the old Countess—she was about sixty-five, but
looked older, from her worn face and plain, almost common style of dress—had refreshed and
amused Josephine very much. While heartily
despising the doctrine, that it is advisable to pull
one's self up in the world by hanging on to the
skirts of great people, she yet had acuteness
enough to see that, both for one's self and one's
children, it is well to cultivate good, suitable,
and pleasant society : not to hide one's head in
a hole, but to see a little of the world, and
choose out of it those friends or acquaintance
from whom we can get, or to whom we can
give, the most sympathy and companionship.

"My girls have no friends at all now," thought

she, "and they will want some. Adrienne must come out this winter; poor little Adrienne!" And she sighed, reflecting that in their present limited circle Miss de Bougainville's "coming out," would be in a very moderate form indeed. "Still she must in time get to know a few people, and she ought to learn to make friends, as Lady Turberville said. If Lady Susan and Lady Emily are like their mother they might be good companions for my poor Adrienne!"

And then the mother's mind wandered off in all sorts of directions, as mothers' minds and hearts always do: to César on his journey to Oxford; to Louis and Martin at school; and back again to her little girls at home. Catherine was still "the baby," and treated as such; but Gabrielle at thirteen looked nearly as womanly as Adrienne. And Gabrielle would certainly grow up beautiful—how beautiful, with her coquettish and impulsive temperament, the mother was almost afraid to think. Still she was se-

D 2

cretly very proud of her, as she was of all her children.

She sat a long time thinking of them, and watching the sun disappear behind the hills, setting in glory upon what seemed to have been the loveliest day of the whole season, and the most enjoyable.

Alas, it was her last day of enjoyment, her last day of peace.

CHAPTER XVI.

SIR EDWARD did not come home till very late that evening, at which his wife was not surprised; he had said that his duties would keep him late, and that he should very likely dine with his brother magistrates afterwards. She concluded he had done so; but when she asked him, he said abruptly No.

"Food, give me some food. And wine too, for I am quite exhausted. You seem as if you took a pleasure in starving me."

Josephine looked up astonished, so irritable was his tone, so wild and worried his look.

"Something has happened. What is it? Is César——"

"You always think of César first, never

of me. Yes, he is all right; he stayed with me and saw me off, before his own train started."

"And you—Edward, is there anything wrong with you?" asked she, taking his hand in a sort of remorse.

But he flung hers off.

"Did I say there was anything wrong? Why do you look at me so? There is nothing the matter with me."

But there was: and by and by she discovered it. A thing which at first he made light of, as of no importance whatever to a gentleman in his position, but which, when little by little she learned its whole bearing, and saw with frightfully clear eyes its possible results, was to Josephine one of those sudden blows which seem often to come upon us poor mortals like thunderbolts, when the air is most still, and there had seemed an hour ago not a cloud in the sky.

Be sure, soon or late, a man's sin will find him out. He, and others for him, may sedulously hide it awhile ; it may appear safely buried, so that no evil consequence can possibly ensue. But, by and by, a bird of the air carries the matter, and in one form or another retribution comes.

By some means—how was never discovered, for Josephine thought she had taken all precautions against such a fatality—that " little bird" began to whisper abroad, not as a public accusation but as a tale of private scandal, how the Reverend Edward Scanlan had wilfully falsified the accounts of the new school at Ditchley, and used for his own benefit the money which had been entrusted to him. And though the charity had suffered no loss, the defalcations being, by some ingenious contrivance, discovered and replaced in time, still the fact remained ; and those people who are always ready to envy a man his sudden prosperity, bruited it abroad from mouth to mouth, till it became the talk of the county.

Curiously enough, the scandal had been a good while in reaching its victims. Sir Edward was not a sensitive man, quick to discover any slight indications of coolness towards himself, and besides, the report had lain smouldering in Ditchley town, where he never went, for weeks before it reached the ears of the country gentlemen, who were mostly staunch old Tories, too proud to listen to the gossip of the lower classes. But having once heard it, and, so far as they could, verified it, they resented in a body this intrusion upon their order, and especially upon the magisterial bench, of a man whom only a lucky chance had saved from the disgrace of a public prosecution. He was in no danger of this now, but, as far as honourable repute went, his character was gone.

"Only think, Josephine," said he, piteously, when he had confessed all to his wife, "all my neighbours gave me the cold shoulder; and one or two of them actually hinted the reason why. Such a fuss about nothing! You paid the money back—did you not?"

" Yes."

" Then what did it matter? These English

people make money their god. Even Lord Turberville, who I thought would protect me---he
had only just come home, and heard nothing of
this unfortunate report till to-day---his lordship
took no notice of me on the bench, and said to
Langhorne, that he thought the wisest thing I
could do would be to send in my resignation
immediately."

"I think so too," said, with white lips, Josephine de Bougainville.

It was no use weeping or complaining. The
miserable man before her needed all her support, all her pity. Under the blow which had
fallen upon him he sank, as usual, utterly crush-
ed and weak---weaker than any woman. Such
men always are.

"They will hunt me down like a hare, these
accursed country squires," moaned he. "I shall
never be able to hold up my head in the county again. And just when I was getting on so
well, and the Turbervilles were come home; and
they might have taken us by the hand and helped us into society. It's very hard!"

"It is hard," said Josephine, beneath her breath; and as she looked round the cheerful drawing-room, so handsome yet so homelike, her whole external possessions, her money, her title, her name, seemed to become valueless. She would have given them all to secure to her children that blessing which, though, thank God, many families have struggled on without it, is yet the safest stronghold and dearest pride of any family—a father's unstained, honourable name.

"But what are we to do, Josephine? Tell me, what are we to do?"

She turned and saw him crouched—all but kneeling at her feet—the man who was tied to her for life; who, with all his faults, was not a deliberate villain, and who now, as was his wont, in his distress took refuge with her, and her alone. For a moment she shrank from him —an expression of pain, unutterable pain—perhaps something worse than pain,---passed over her face, and then she feebly smiled.

"I cannot answer you at once. Give me time to think."

"Very well. Only, Josephine, do remember what your poor husband has suffered this day. For God's sake do not you be unkind to me!"

"No, I will not. It is for God's sake," she repeaetd to herself, with a deep meaning; almost as deep and earnest as a prayer.

During her many hours of solitary musings— more numerous now than ever in her life—Josephine had learnt much. That burning sense of wrong—wrong done to herself and her children by their father, had in some measure died out: she looked upon him sorrowfully, as being chiefly his own enemy: she could protect both them and herself from him now. And in another way her mind had changed; she begun dimly to guess at the solemn truth, without which all life becomes a confused haze ;—that what we do for people is not for themselves, or for ourselves, but for something higher. Thus it was for God's sake, not for his own, that she resolved to hold fast to her husband.

"Edward," she said, "indeed I never mean to be unkind to you; but this is a terrible grief to me. To be sure, the thing is not much worse known than unknown, except so far as it affects the children. Had César any idea of it, do you think?"

"Yes—no. Well, yes; I told him something of it," stammered Sir Edward. "I had nobody else to speak to, and he saw how broken-down and upset I was. Poor fellow! he insisted on seeing me safe off home before he started himself for Oxford. I must say César behaved very well to me to-day."

"My good boy!" muttered the mother; and then with a thrill of maternal suffering at how he might suffer—"Oh, my poor César!"

"César—always César! Can't you for one moment think of me?"

Ay, that was the key to this man's life. He had never thought but of himself, and himself alone. Such an one—and oh! what hundreds there are like him!—ought never to be either husband or father.

Josephine turned grave reproachful eyes upon him—the deadweight who had dragged her down all her days. It always had been so—apparently it was to be so to the end.

"Edward, consider a little, and you will find I do think of you: but there is plenty of time. We have no need to do anything in haste—if indeed," with a sigh, "anything remains to be done."

And there came helplessly the thought upon her of how little could be done. A lie she could have fought against; but there was no fighting against the truth. In a gentle way she said as much.

"True or not, Josephine, I'll not bear it. Am I, with all my Irish talent, to be a byword among these clodhopping English Squires? They hate me because I am Irish. I always knew that. But I'll soon teach them differently. I, with my wealth, could take a position wherever I pleased. We'll leave this place immediately."

"Leave this place?"

"And I shall be only too glad of the opportunity to quit this horrid old house; you know I always disliked it. We can't sell it, more's the pity! but we could easily let it, and we will."

"We will not," said Josephine, roused to desperation.

"But I say we will, and I am master here!" cried Sir Edward violently. "I have been planning it the whole way home," added he, more pacifically, as he saw that his wrath had not the slightest effect upon his wife. It only tightened the shut lips, and gave an added paleness to the steady, firm features. "We can give out that your health requires us to winter abroad, and go quietly away in a week or two. Once gone, we need never come back any more."

"Never come back any more? When I loved the place so: when I had settled down here for life, and was so happy!—so happy! Husband, you are very cruel to me! And heaven is cruel too. My troubles are more than I can bear."

She sat down, wringing her hands. A kind
of despair came over her—the sudden re-action
which we often feel when trouble follows a lull
of peace—as sharp as the first chill of returning
winter. But we get accustomed to it presently.
So did she.

Against this scheme of her husband's—very
natural to him, for his first thought in any difficulty was to run away—Lady de Bougainville
at first rebelled with all her might. She refused
point-blank to quit her home—though she were
ignored by the whole county, and though the
arrows of evil tongues were to fly around her
head as thick as hail.

"I am not afraid; I have done nothing,"
she said haughtily. "No possible blame can
attach to the children or me. And, even with
regard to what has been, since nobody was
really injured, and it will never happen again.
would it not be possible to remain and live it
down?"

So reasoned she with Mr. Langhorne, who
was the only person whom in her extremity she

took counsel of: confessed the whole thing, and asked him what he thought would be the wisest course.

"For my children's sake—my children, you see," pleaded the poor mother. Of herself she cared nothing; would gladly have hidden her head anywhere in merciful obscurity. "Had I not better stay here and brave it out? Nobody could bring up the tale so as to harm the children?"

Mr. Langhorne hesitated. He knew the world better than she did. Still, she was so bent upon remaining, that she resisted him as much as she did her husband; who, cowed by her determined will, assumed the air of a much-injured, and most patient man, told her to "have it all her own way; he should never say another word on the subject."

But he did though: reverting to it day after day with the worrying persistency of a weak soul that tries by every underhand means to shake a stronger one. Alas! only too often succeeding.

For a few weeks Lady de Bougainville bore all her misery at home, all her slights abroad—some imaginary, perhaps; but others real enough. For the taint of "something dishonourable" attached to a family—especially in a thinly populated country district, ignorant of the tricks of trade, great or small, which are practised in larger communities—is a thing not easily removed. Long after its exact circumstances are forgotten, the vague stigma remains. In proportion to his former popularity, his old parishioners, and indeed the whole county, now viewed with extreme severity the Reverend Sir Edward de Bougainville.

Several times Josephine drove purposely to Ditchley, showing her face to the world at large, and calling upon the people she knew; but they were all rather cold to her, and some barely civil. Lady Turberville, whom she one day accidentally met, though not uncourteous —for the old lady stopped to speak to her, and had a tone of sympathy in her voice—still made not the slightest inquiry after Sir Ed-

ward, and gave no hint of the proposed visit
of the Ladies Susan and Emily to Oldham
Court. In short, that slight untangible coolness, that "sending to Coventry," which in a
provincial neighbourhood is, socially, the ruin
of any family, had obviously befallen the De
Bougainvilles. Once begun, these things always increase rather than diminish; and however she might shut her eyes to it, Josephine
could not help seeing before her and hers a
future of splendid loneliness, duller and drearier
even than poverty.

Then, too, an uncomfortable change. physical
and mental, came over her husband. The shock
of his sudden fortunes had thrown him into a
rather excited condition. He had been top-
heavy with prosperity, so to speak, and against
this sudden bleak wind of adversity he could
not fight at all. He fell into a low way, refused to do anything or go anywhere, and sat
all day long shivering over the fire, bemoaning
his hard lot, and complaining that the world
was all against him, as it had been from his

youth up. He could not bear his wife out of his sight, yet when she was in it he was always scolding her, saying she was killing him by inches in keeping him at Oldham Court.

"Can it be really so? What is the matter with him?" she asked of Dr. Waters, whom she had at last secretly summoned—for Sir Edward refused all medical advice, saying that the sight of a doctor was as good, or as bad, as a death-warrant.

Dr. Waters made no immediate reply. Perhaps he really had none to give. That mysterious disease called softening of the brain, which seems to attack the weakest and the strongest brains—letting the lucky mediocre ones go free—was then unnamed in medical science; yet I think, by all accounts, its earliest symptoms must even then have been developing in Josephine's husband. She knew it not. nobody knew it; but its results were painful enough, throwing a cloud of gloom over the whole family. And upon this state of things

E 2

the younger boys—planning their first Christmas at Oldham Court, yule-logs and guisards,
according to the merry Christmas-keeping of
all the wealthy families in the county—came
ignorantly home. César too—but César was
not ignorant, though in all his letters he had
never yet said a word of what he knew. He
only held his mother's hand sometimes, and
followed her tenderly about the house, and
made things as easy for her as he could; but
he seemed to think—it was his nature, and had
been his grandfather's, too, she remembered—
that the easiest thing was silence.

"Perhaps, after all," said Dr. Waters on his
second visit, "it would be better to go."

"To leave home, you mean, as my husband
wishes—for a time?"

"Yes, for a time," repeated the doctor with
his eyes cast down. "Long or short, as may
be advisable. Change of scene, without delay,
is, I think, very necessary for Sir Edward. And
for the boys, they have but a dull life here. You
will return in triumph," added he cheerfully, "in

time to have an ox roasted whole, and all sorts
of rejoicings when César comes of age."

Lady de Bougainville turned sharply away.
How all her delights had crumbled down to
dust and ashes! Alas, to what sort of an in-
heritance would he come, her handsome young
heir? And who would stand up and wish him
the heir's best benediction, that he might tread
in his father's footsteps all his days?

Nevertheless, she could but follow where fate
led, and do the best that seemed possible for the
time being. So standing at her favourite oriel
window, looking down the straight evergreen
alleys of her beloved garden, where the holly-
berries shone scarlet in the winter sun, and the
arbutus trees were glittering under the first
white dust of snow, she made up her mind to
leave Oldham Court; to slip the dear safe an-
chor of home, and go drifting about upon the
wide world.

Some may count this a very small thing—a
very infinitesimal sacrifice; but I know better.
However it was made; and having once put her

hand to the plough she never looked back, but drove it straight through her pleasant flowers with a firm remorseless hand.

Of course her husband was delighted. She had come to her senses at last, and he congratulated her accordingly. He laid plan after plan of what he should like best to do, what would amuse him most; and at last thought that considering it was winter time, and rather too early for the London season, it would be well to adopt a suggestion which somebody or other threw out, and take a tour through the cathedral towns of England.

"You see, this will be particularly suitable for me in my character of a clergyman." For since politics and the Earl of Turberville had lost their charm he went back upon that, and became once more stricter than ever in his religious observances.

Josephine cared little where she went. So, mostly by chance, the thing was decided. They were to begin with Canterbury.

"But you don't want to take the children with

us, my dear?" said Sir Edward querulously. " I shall have no pleasure at all if I am bothered with a lot of children at my heels." So Josephine gave this up too.

Her last few days at Oldham Court, appeared, she herself once told me, to have fled exactly like a dream. The whole thing was done suddenly:—leaving the children behind in charge of the good governess and Bridget. She intended to come back and shut up the house, for she obstinately refused to let it; but still, when the carriage slowly ascended the hilly road, and she looked down on the grey gables nestling in sunshine in the valley below, she had a fatal foreboding that she should never see Oldham Court again. She never did.

I do not mean to make any pathetic scene out of all this. Many persons might say that Lady de Bougainville's regrets on the subject were mere morbid imagination, when she had so many tangible blessings left her to enjoy. It might be, and yet I pity her, and can understand how she fell into a kind of dull despon-

dency, very unusual for her, which lasted for
several days.

Out of it she was roused by a chance incident;
one of those small things which are often the
pivot upon which much greater things turn.
Wandering round Canterbury cathedral aimlessly
enough—for Sir Edward took little interest in
ecclesiastical architecture, and was much more
interested in finding out where the Deanery
was, and whether he ought not to call upon the
Dean, whom he had once met, and who would
probably ask them to dinner—Lady de Bougainville came upon the queer old door leading to that portion of the crypt which, ever
since the revolution of the Edict of Nantes
—indeed, I believe, earlier still—has been
assigned by law and custom to the use of the
French Protestants whose forefathers had taken
refuge in England. While asking a question
or two of the verger, she dimly recollected
having heard of the place before. Her father
had once "assisted" at a Sunday service there,
and described it to her. Keenly interested, she

tried to peer through the cracks in the door
and the spidery windows: little was to be seen,
but she managed to catch a few glimpses of the
interior, the low arched ceiling, white-washed
like the walls; the plain, common wooden pews
and pulpit, whereon lay a book, torn and worm-
eaten—a centuries-old French Huguenot Bible
—for she could read the words " Saincte Ecri-
ture" on the open title-page.

A strange contrast it was, this poor, plain—
pathetically plain—little conventicle, to the
magnificent cathedral overhead where she had
just been hearing service ; but it suited her present state of mind exactly. Sickened of wealth,
feeling the hollowness of the sham religion about
her, her heart seemed to spring back like an
over-bent bow to the noble poverty of her childish days, to the rigid uncompromising faith of
her French forefathers.

" Every Sunday they have service here, you
say?" she asked of the verger. " Edward,
shall we go to-morrow? I should like it very
much."

"I daresay : you always do like common and ungenteel places. No, I would not be seen there upon any account."

"No matter," she thought, "I will go alone." And next day, while her husband was taking a long sleep, she sallied forth through the rainy streets; wrapping herself up in her cloak, and trudging on, almost as Mrs. Scanlan used to trudge in days gone by. No fear, she thought, of her being recognized as Lady de Bougainville.

And yet, as she passed under the low door of the crypt, entering side by side with that small and rather queer-looking congregation, chiefly French artificers of various sorts, with their wives and families, descendants of the early *émigrés* or later comers into the town, who, but for this ancient institution of service under the cathedral, would probably long ago have forgotten their religion and race, and become altogether amalgamated with the inhabitants of Canterbury; when she looked at them, and heard in faint whispers their tongue of another land, as they noticed the rare presence of a stranger among them, Josephine began to feel strange stirrings in her heart.

It is curious, as we advance in middle life, especially when there is a great gulf between that life and our childish one, how sharp and distinct the latter grows! For years, except in her children's caressing chatter, Josephine had scarcely heard the sound of her native tongue— that is, her ancestors' tongue, for, as I have said, she herself had been born after her parents quitted France; nor since childhood had she been in any place of worship like that which her father used to take her to—a bare meeting-house, rough as this, of which it strongly reminded her. When she sat down, it almost seemed as if the old Vicomte sat beside her with his gentle " *Sois sage, ma petite fille.*" And when the minister, in his high French intonation, a little " singsong" and long drawn out, began to read " *L'Evangile selon Sainte Jean, chapitre premier. La parole était au commencement: la Parole était avec Dieu, et la Parole était*

Dieu," old times came back upon her so forcibly
that it was with difficulty she could restrain
her tears.

What the congregation thought of her she
knew not, cared not. Possibly, for many Sundays after, those simple people talked of and
looked for the strange lady who that Sunday
had worshipped with them—whether Frenchwoman or Englishwoman they could not tell,
only that she had left in the alms-box several
bright English sovereigns, which helped on the
poor of the flock through a very hard winter.
She came and she went, speaking to nobody,
and nobody venturing to speak to her, but the
influence of those two hours effected in her
mind a complete revolution.

"I will go home," she said to herself, as she
walked back through Canterbury streets, still
in the pelting rain; "home to my father's faith
and my father's people, if any of them yet remain. I will bring up my children not English, but French; after the noble old Huguenot pattern, such as my father used to tell me

of, and such as he was himself. *Mon père, mon père!*"

It was a dream, of course, springing out of her entire ignorance; as Utopian as many another fancy which she had cherished, only to see it melt away like a breaking wave; still at present it was forced so strongly upon her mind that it gave her a gleam of new hope. [Almost as soon as she returned to the hotel, she proposed to her husband, with feigned carelessness, for he now generally objected to anything which he saw she had set her heart upon—that instead of continuing their tour in this gloomy weather, they should at once send for the children, cross the Channel, and spend the New Year in Paris, *le jour de l'an* being such a very amusing time.

"Is it?" said Sir Edward, catching at the notion. "And I want amusing so much! Yes. I think I should like to go. How soon could we start?"

"I think, within a week."

She despised herself for humouring him; for

leading him by means of his whims instead of
his reason to needful ends, but she was often
obliged to do both now. A curious kind of art-
fulness, and childish irritability mingled with
senile obstinacy, often seized him ; when he was
very difficult to manage, he who as a young
man had been so pleasant and good-tempered,
in truth, a better temper than she.   But things
were different now.

Ere her husband could change his mind,
which he was apt to do, and ere the novelty of
the fresh idea wore off, Lady de Bougainville
hastily made all her arrangements, left Oldham
Court in the hands of Mr. Langhorne ; sent for
her children and some of her servants, and almost before she recognised the fact herself, was
in the land of her forefathers, the very city
where more than one of the last generation of
them had expiated on the guillotine the crime
of having been noble, in the best sense of the
word, for centuries.

As Josephine drove through the streets in
the chilly winter dusk, she thought with a

curious fancy—how her father must have looked, wakened early one morning, a poor crying child, to see the death-cart, with his father in it, go by;—and again, with a shudder, how her beautiful great-aunt must have felt when the cold steel first touched her neck. Ah! but those were terrible times, to be so near behind us as seventy years!

Paris, such as Lady de Bougainville then saw it, and as long afterwards she used to describe it to me, lingering with the loving garrulousness of age upon things, and places, and people, all swept away into the gulf of the past—ancient Paris exists no more. Imperial "improvements" so-called, have swept away nearly all its historical landmarks, and made it, what probably its present ruler most desired it should be made, a city without a history. When I visited it myself, wishful as I was to retrace the steps of our dear old friend, and tell her on our return about these places she knew, we could find almost none of them. Except the quaint old Rue St. Honoré, where in an hotel, half French, half

English, which Sir Edward took a fancy to, she lived during her whole residence there.

I knew not if it were the stirring of the mercurial ancestral blood, or merely the bright, clear, sunshiny atmosphere, but Lady de Bougainville felt her heart lighter as soon as she entered Paris. She was not one to mourn over the inevitable ; Oldham Court was left behind, but she had many pleasant things surrounding her still. She went sight-seeing almost every morning with her happy children, and of afternoons she took her daily drive with Sir Edward, showing him everything she could think of to amuse him—and he really was amused for the time. His health and spirits revived ; he confessed Paris was a pleasant place to winter in, or would be, as soon as they came to know people, and to be known. With this end in view he haunted Galignani's, and was on the watch for all the English visitors to the hotel, in case some of their names might be familiar to him.

But in Paris, as in London, came the same

difficulty inevitable under the circumstances. Socially the De Bougainvilles had not yet risen to the level of their money, and beyond a certain point it helped them little. They were almost as lonely, and as entirely without acquaintances, in the Rue St. Honoré as they had been in St. James's Street. Vainly did Sir Edward harry his wife's memory for the name of every noble family with whom her father had had to do, hoping to hunt them out and thrust himself upon them. Vainly, too, did he urge her to leave a card at the British Embassy, or even at the Tuileries, for one De Bougainville had been about fifty years ago a very faithful friend to one of the Orleans family. But something— was it pride or was it shame, or perhaps merely natural reticence ?—made Josephine steadily and firmly decline these back-stairs methods of getting into society.

César, too, who was nearly grown up now, had a great dislike to the thing. "Mamma," he would say, "if people do not seek us of their own accord, and for ourselves, I had ·rather have no friends or acquaintance at all. We can do very well without them."

" I think so too," said Lady de Bougainville. But she did not perplex herself much about the matter. She knew the lack was only temporary. Every time she looked at her son, who, to his natural grace was daily adding that air of manliness and gentlemanliness which the associations of University life give to almost every young fellow, more or less, she smiled to herself with perfect content. There was no fear of her César's not making friends everywhere by and by.

He was her consolation for a good many things which she found difficult to bear. Not great things ; she had no heavy troubles now ; but little vexations. It was sometimes very trying to watch the slight shrugs or covert smiles with which the civil Frenchmen he met at *tables d'hote*, theatres, &c., commented silently on the brusquerie or " bumptiousness" of the rich *milord Anglais*, who was always asserting his right to the best of everything, For in a

foreign country, more patent than ever becomes
the fact that, however his rank or wealth, no
thoroughly selfish man ever is, or even appears,
a gentleman.

Rich as Sir Edward was, he found that when
one's only key to society is a golden one, it takes
a good while to fit it in. He was growing weary
of the delay, and speculating whether it would
not be well to leave Paris, when the magic
"open sesame" to his heart's desire arrived in a
very unexpected way.

With a vague yearning after her father's
faith, dimly as she understood it, a restless seeking after something upon which to stay her
soul, sickened with the religious hollowness
amidst which she had lived so long, Josephine
went, Sunday after Sunday, to the French Pro-
testant Chapel. Not that the preacher could
teach much—few preachers can, to hearers like
herself, whose sharp experience of life mocks
all dogmatising as mere idle words ; it is God
only who can bring faith to a soul which has lost
all faith in man. But she liked to listen to the

mellifluous French of the good old minister—
liked too the simplicity of the service, and the
evident earnestness of the congregation. An
earnestness quite different from that of the wor-
shippers she saw in Catholic churches, though this
was touching too. She often envied those poor
kneeling women praying even to a Saint or a
Holy Virgin in whom they could believe.

But these French Protestants seemed to worship God as she thought He would best desire
to be worshipped—open-eyed, fearless-hearted,
after the pattern of their forefathers and
hers, persecuted and hunted to death, yet
never renouncing Him. The difference, so
difficult to understand, between faith and su-
perstition, was there still. She often fancied
that in these nineteenth-century faces she
could still detect gleams of the old Huguenot
spirit, with its strength, its courage, its un-
paralleled self-devotion. A spirit as different
from that of Catholic France as that of the
Puritans and Covenanters was from that corrupt
Court of the Stuarts.

She was in a dream of this kind, such as she fell into almost every Sunday; when looking up she saw among these strange faces a face she knew; and as soon as the service was over, she hurried after the person, who was Priscilla Nunn.

"How came you here! Who would have expected it? My good Priscilla, I am so glad to see you—so very glad!"

The woman curtsied, looking pleased, said she had watched " my Lady " for several Sundays, but thought perhaps my Lady did not care to notice her. That she had given up business and gone back to her old profession, and was now living as nurse and humble companion with Lady Emma Lascelles.

"She is very ill, my Lady : will never be better. She often speaks of you. Shall I tell her I saw you?"

"No—yes," hesitated Josephine, for she had been a little wounded by Lady Emma's long silence, which, however, this illness explained. She stood perplexed, but still cordially holding

Priscilla by the hand, when she saw her husband
waiting for her in the carriage, and watching
her with astonished suspicious eyes. Hastily she
gave her address, and joined him; for she knew
well what vials of wrath would be poured out
upon her devoted head. As was really the case,
until Sir Edward discovered with whom the obnoxious Priscilla was living.

"Lady Emma! Then you must at once call
upon her. She may be of the greatest service
to you. She used to be so very fond of you.
Where is she residing?"

Josephine had never asked, but her pride or
reticence was rendered needless by Mr. Lascelles' appearing the very next day to entreat
her to visit his wife, who was longing to see
her.

So, without more ado, Lady de Bougainville
put on her bonnet as rapidly as Mrs. Scanlan
used to do, and went alone, a street's length, to
the quiet faubourg, where, surrounded by all
Parisian elegance and luxury, the young creature who had once come to Ditchley as a bride

lay fading away. She had lost child after child
—hopes rising only to be blighted; and now,
apparently in a decline, was slipping peacefully
out of a world which upon her had opened so
brightly and closed so soon. Yet she still took
her usual warm human interest in it, and was
exceedingly glad to see again Lady de Bougainville.

"An old friend with a new face," she said
smiling; "but nothing would ever alter you.
I am glad my cousin left you all his money; nobody else wanted it, and you can make good
use of it, and enjoy it too. You have your
children." And poor Lady Emma burst into
tears.

After this the two women renewed all their
former intimacy; and as Mr. Lascelles knew
everybody, and surrounded his wife with as
many pleasant people as he could think of to
amuse her, it so happened that this mere chance,
occurring through such a humble medium as
Priscilla Nunn, furnished the means by which
the De Bougainvilles entered into Parisian so-

ciety. Really good society, such as even Sir
Edward approved, for it included people of
higher rank than in his wildest ambition he had
ever expected to mix with.

The Court, then resident at Paris, must have
been, so long as it lasted, one of the best and
purest Courts which France has ever known.
Whatever its political mistakes or misfortunes,
domestically it was without alloy. No one
could enter the household circle of the citizen-
king without admiring and loving it. High-
toned, yet simple; fond of art and literature,
yet rating moral worth above both these; com-
bining the old aristocratic grace with the liber-
alism of the time, and assigning to rank, wealth,
talent, each its fitting place and due honour,—
though many years have elapsed since its disper-
sion and downfall, all those now living who
knew it speak tenderly of the Court of Louis
Philippe.

Lady de Bougainville did, to her very last
hour. Whether she "shone" therein, I cannot
tell—she never said so; but she keenly enjoyed

it. More, certainly, than her husband, who, after his first flush of delight, found himself a little out of his element there. He could not understand the perfect simplicity of those great people, who could associate with poor authors and artists upon equal terms; who were friendly and kind to their servants; and who, instead of going about all day with allegorical crowns on their heads, were in reality very quiet persons, who would condescend to the commonest things and pursuits—such as shocked much a grand personage like Sir Edward de Bougainville. He was altogether puzzled, and sometimes a little uncomfortable; finally he held aloof, and let his wife go into society alone, or with the companionship of her daughter.

Adrienne "came out." Sitting beside her beautiful mother, as shy and silent as any French demoiselle, but much amused by what she saw around her; she looked on, taking little share in the gay world, until she saw herself put forward as a desirable "*partie*" by an energetic French mother, when she turned in frightened appeal to her own, and the "*pretendu*" was speedily extinguished. Nevertheless, in spite of her plain looks, and defect in figure, the reported large "*dot*" of Mademoiselle de Bougainville attracted several chances of marriage: to which Adrienne was as indifferent as her mother could desire.

But henceforth, Josephine often thought with some anxiety of this dear child so unlike herself, so unfit to battle with the world. Shrinking, timid, easily led and influenced, Adrienne inherited much from her father, and almost nothing from her mother, except her uprightness and sincerity.

"If you do marry," Lady de Bougainville sometimes said to her, "it must be some one who will be very good to you, some one whom I can entirely trust, or I shall break my heart. Sometimes I hope, my darling, that you will not marry at all."

"Very likely not, mamma," Adrienne would answer, blushing brightly. "I certainly would rather not marry a Frenchman."

So the mother rested content that none of these gay young fellows, who, she felt sure, only sought her for her money, had touched the heart of her young daughter, whom she still called fondly her " little " girl.

CHAPTER XVII.

WHEN they had been a year at Paris, or near it—for in the fashionable season for " *la campagne* " they drifted with the usual Parisian crowd to some place sufficiently in reach of the city not to be dull—Sir Edward began to suggest moving on. There was a curious restlessness about him which made him never settle anywhere. Back to Oldham Court he positively refused to go; and when the subject was fairly entered upon, Josephine found that her son César had the same repugnance. He and she had never spoken together of that fatal rumour which had been the secret cause of their sudden departure, but that the proud, honest, reticent boy knew it, and felt it acutely, she was well aware. ·

"No, mother," he said, when she consulted with him, for she had already learnt to rest upon his premature wisdom and good sense; "don't let us go back to Oldham Court,—at least not for some years. The house will take no harm, and the land is well let; Mr. Langhorne, last time he was at Oxford, told me that you will be richer by letting it than living at it; and I don't want to live there—never again! Besides," hastening to heal up a wound he thought he had made, "you see, I must be a busy man, must enter a profession, work my way up in the world, and earn my own fortune. Then, mother darling, you shall have Oldham Court for your dower-house, when you are an old lady."

She smiled, and ceased urging her point, though she was pining for a settled resting-place. At last César saw this, and went hunting about England on pedestrian tours till he succeeded in finding a place that he felt sure she would like, and his father too—a large, old fashioned mansion; not Gothic, but belonging

to the time of Queen Anne; fallen into much
dis-repair, but still capable of being revived
into its original splendour.

"And you will have quite money enough to
do this, Mr. Langhorne says," added the prudent boy. "And the doing of it would amuse
papa so much. Besides, it is such a beautiful
old place; and oh, what a park! what trees!
Then the rooms are so lofty, and large, and
square. You might give such dinners and balls
—I like a ball, you know. Dearest mother,
please think twice before you throw overboard
our chance of Brierley Hall."

She promised, though with little interest in
the matter—as little interest as we sometimes
take in places or people which are to be our
destiny. And Oldham Court—which she loved
so, which she had set her heart upon—she fore-
saw, only too clearly, would never be her home
any more.

Still, she would have done almost anything
to please César, who was growing up her
heart's delight. He only came to Paris on

passing visits, being quite taken up with his Oxford life, in which his earnest perseverance atoned for any lack of brilliant talents; and he worked for his degree like any poor lad, forgetting he was heir to a wealthy gentleman, and scarcely even remembering his twenty-first birthday, which passed by without any oxen roasted whole or other external rejoicings—except the joy of his mother that he was now a man, with his career safe in his own hands.

César was after all more of an Englishman than a Frenchman, even in spite of his resemblance to his grandfather, so strong that more than one old courtier had come up to him and welcomed the descendant of M. le Vicomte de Bougainville. But the young fellow added to his English gravity that charming French grace which we Britons often lack, and his tall figure and handsome looks made him noticeable in every *salon* where he appeared.

His proud mother had especially remarked this on one evening which had a painful close.

It was a *reception*, whither she and her son went alone together—Sir Edward having desired that Adrienne would remain at home and play dominoes with him—since he had been in France he had taken greatly to that harmless game, which seemed to suit him exactly. And Adrienne had obeyed, a little reluctantly, as the reception was at a house where, timid as she was, she liked to go. For the hostess was a lady who, though too poor to "entertain" as we English understand the word—indeed, Sir Edward complained bitterly that he never got anything at her reunions but biscuits and weak raspberry vinegar—yet, by her exquisite tact and cultivated grace, which is often better than talent in a woman, succeeded in gathering around her once a week all the notable people in Paris. As Lady de Bougainville stood in the midst of the assemblage, with César at her side, I could imagine that mother and son were a good sight to behold, both by one another, and by the brilliant throng around them.

"Still, we ought to go home," she whispered

to him, more than once, even while giving herself up, half Frenchwoman as she was, to the enjoyment of the minute, allowing herself to rest, gay and at ease, on the summit of one of those sunshiny waves which are for ever rising and falling in most human lives. "I should like to return even sooner than we promised, in case papa might be a little dull. He told me that he was to be quite alone at home tonight."

"Indeed!" said César, dryly. "I thought I overheard him giving orders about a little supper that was to be prepared for some visitor he expected. But," added the lad, with meaning, "papa often—forgets."

"César!" said Lady de Bougainville, sharply; and then—almost with a kind of entreaty, "Do not be hard upon your father."

The mother and son came home at once, though it was half an hour before they were expected and, apparently, wanted. For there, sitting opposite to Sir Edward, playing dominoes with him, and amusing him till he burst into

shouts of laughter, which were faintly echoed
by Adrienne—who hung about the two, looking
as happy and delighted as she used to do of
evenings at Wren's Nest—was the object of
Josephine's long dislike and dread—Mr. Summerhayes.

There are women, justifiably the aversion of
their husband's male friends; rigidly righteous,
and putting virtue forward in such an obnoxious manner, that vice seems less unpleasant by
comparison. These I do not uphold. But I do
uphold a woman who dares to call wickedness
by its right name, and shut her door upon it,
however charming it may be ; who, like David,
" hates all evil doers," and will not let them
" continue in her sight." Poor King David—a
sinner too ! But if he sinned, he also repented.
And, had *he* repented, I doubt not Lady de Bougainville would have been the first to hold out
a kindly hand even to Mr. Summerhayes.

As it was, she made no pretence of the sort.
She stood—her hand unextended, her eyes fixed on her husband's guest with a grave astou-

ishment. So unmistakeable was her manner, so strong her determination, that Summerhayes made no attempt to counteract either, but saying "I perceive I am intruding here," bowed and departed.

His friend never attempted to detain him, but burst into bitter complaint when he was gone.

"Josephine, how can you be so unkind, so rude? You have driven away the only friend I have—the only fellow whose company is amusing to me, or whom I care to see in all Paris."

"Have you seen him often?"

"Why, yes—no; not so very often. And only at Galignani's. I never brought him here before to-night."

"Then, I entreat you, do not bring him here again. You know what he is, and what I think of him. Into this house, and among my young sons and daughters, that man shall never come. Another time, when I happen to be absent, will you remember that, Edward?"

She spoke strongly—more strongly perhaps than she should have spoken to their father in her children's presence; but it was necessary. Indecision might have been fatal. They were too old to be left in the dark as to their associates.

No one answered her. César, who had looked as vexed as she, took up a book and walked away to bed; but Adrienne followed her mother to her room, greatly agitated.

"Indeed, Mamma, I had no idea Mr. Summerhayes was coming till he came. And I was so pleased to see him. I did not know you disliked him so much."

That was true, for she had said as little as possible about him to her young daughter; his delinquencies were of a kind not so easy to speak of to a girl, and of a man known to the family as their father's friend. Even now she hardly knew how to explain with safety the motives of her conduct.

"I do dislike him, Adrienne, and I have just cause, as I will tell you by and by, if necessary.

At present let us put the matter aside. Mr. Summerhayes is not likely to come here again ; Papa says he shall not invite him."

But she knew none the less that she would have to take all imaginable precaution against the thing she dreaded—against the father, who was no sort of guard over his own children— who, when he liked or wished a thing, would stoop to any underhand means of accomplishing it. For, as she afterwards discovered, her husband had all along kept up a desultory correspondence with Mr. Sumerhayes, who, though not actually supplying him with money—Sir Edward since his accession to wealth having grown extremely parsimonious—he had allowed to make use of him in various ways which flattered his vanity and his love of patronizing; and at last in one way which, when Josephine found it out, she opened her eyes in horrified astonishment.

"He marry Adrienne?" And when Sir Edward one day showed her rather hesitatingly a letter making formally that request, she tore it up in a fit of unrestrainable passion. "How dare he! Of course you refused him at once ?"

"I—I did not quite like to do that. He is acquainted with all my affairs. Oh, Josephine, pray—pray be careful."

The old story! The strong, wicked man, knowing his power over the weak one, and using it. At a glance Lady de Bougainville saw the whole thing.

"Coward!" she was near saying, and then her sudden blind fury died down : it was dangerous. She needed to keep her eyes open, her mind calm, and all her wits about her. In a new and utterly unexpected form the old misery had risen up again. Once more she had to protect her children, not only from Mr. Summerhayes, but from their own father.

"And when did you receive this letter, Edward ?" she asked, not passionately now, and he was blunt to anything else.

"A week ago. But I was afraid you might not approve ; Adrienne is so young."

"Adrienne will have money. She would be a very convenient wife for Mr. Summerhayes."

"And Summerhayes has talent, and is of good family, and he has sown his wild oats, he tells me, long ago. He might suit her very well. You had better let him take her. It is not everyone who would marry poor Adrienne. And all women ought to be married, you know."

"Ought they?"

"Come, come, I am glad to see you so reasonable. Who shall answer the letter, you or I?"

"I will."

"And you'll give the man a chance? You'll not make an enemy of him?"

"Has he ever spoken to the child? But no, Adrienne would have told me—she always tells her mother everything." And the comfort which always came with the thought of her children soothed the mother's half-maddened spirit. "If he has held his tongue, I—I will forgive him. But he must never see my daughter's face again."

And to this effect she wrote, her husband looking over her shoulder the while.

"Don't offend him, please don't offend him," was all Sir Edward said. When his wife looked as she looked now, he was so utterly cowed, that he never risked any open opposition.

Whether to tell Adrienne what had happened, and how her parents, knowing what Mr. Summerhayes was, had decided for her at once, and so put her on her guard against him, or else by complete silence avoid the risk of awakening in the impressible heart of seventeen a tender interest for a possibly ill-used and merely unfortunate man : this was the question which the mother argued within herself twenty times a day. At length she left it for circumstances to decide, and simply kept watch—incessant watch.

Mr. Summerhayes played his cards well. He did not attempt to come to the house again ; he made no open demonstrations of any kind,

but he followed Adrienne at a distance with
that silent, sedulous worship which even so
innocent a creature could hardly help perceiving. By using the name and influence of Sir
Edward, he got the *entrée* into several houses
where the De Bougainvilles visited, and there,
though he never addressed her, he watched
Adrienne ceaselessly with his melancholy poetical eyes. True, he was forty, and she seventeen; but these ages are sometimes mutually
attractive, and as a child she had been very
fond of Mr. Summerhayes. Often, her mother
recollected, he had taken her on his knee and
called her his little wife. Many a true word is
spoken in jest. Now that the years had
dwindled down between them—leaving him
still attractive, still youthful-looking—for people
with neither hearts nor consciences are sometimes very slow in growing old—did Adrienne
remember all this?

She was so quiet, so exceedingly quiet, that
her mother had no means of guessing at her
feelings. Since she learnt that he was disliked,

Adrienne had never uttered Mr. Summerhayes' name. When they met him in society, they passed him with a mere bow of recognition, for Lady de Bougainville did not wish to go proclaiming him as a scoundrel to everybody, and desired above all to avoid every appearance of injustice or malice towards him : only she guarded with ceaseless care her own lamb from every advance of the smiling wolf. Who gradually conducted himself so little like a wolf, and so like an ordinary man of society, that her fears died down, and she began to hope that after all they had been exaggerated.

Until one day when the climax came.

The man must have been mad or blind—blind with self-esteem, or maddened by the desperation of his circumstances, before he did such a thing ; but one Sunday morning he sent to Miss de Bougainville a bouquet and a letter. Not an actual offer of marriage, but something so very near it, that the simplest maiden of seventeen could be under no mistake as to what he meant.

Only, like many a man of the world, he a little overshot his mark by calculating too much upon this simplicity; for Adrienne, trembling, confused, hardly knowing what she did, but yet impelled by her tender conscience and her habit of perfect candour, came at once and put the letter into her mother's hands.

Lady de Bougainville read it through twice before she spoke. It was a clever letter, very clever; one of those which Mr. Summerhayes was particularly apt at writing. It put forward his devotion in the most humble, and most disinterested light; it claimed for his love the paternal sanction; and, in the only thing wherein he transgressed the bounds of decorum, namely in asking her to meet him in the quiet galleries of the Louvre, that Sunday afternoon—he put himself under the shelter of her father, who had promised him, he said, to bring her there.

Twice, as I said, in wrath that was utterly dumb, Josephine read this letter, and then looking up she caught sight of Adrienne's burning face, agitated by a new and altogether incomprehensible emotion.

"My child," she cried, "oh, my poor child!"

To say that she would rather have seen Adrienne in her grave than married to Mr. Summerhayes, is a form of phrase which many foolish parents have used and lived to repent of. Lady de Bougainville was too wise to use it at all, or to neutralize by any extravagance of expression a truth which seemed to her clear as daylight,—would be clear even to the poor child herself if only it were put before her.

"Adrienne," she said sorrowfully, "I am glad you showed me this letter. It is, as you may see, equivalent to an offer of marriage, which you will refuse like the rest, I hope. You do not really care for Mr. Summerhayes?"

Adrienne hung her head. "I have known him all my life—and—he likes me so."

"But he is a bad man; a worse man than you know or have any idea of."

"He has been: but he tells me, you see, that I should make him better."

The old delusion! Unfortunate child!

Adrienne's mother had now no alternative. Terrible as it was to open her young daughter's eyes, the thing must be done. Better a sharp pain and over; better any present anguish than years of life-long misery.

For, even granting there was one grain of truth under the man's false words, Josephine scouted altogether the theory of doing evil that good may come. In the goodness of a man who is only kept good by means of a gratified passion, she altogether disbelieved. Strong as the love of woman is to guide an erring man, to settle and control a vacillating one; over a thoroughly vicious one it has almost no effect, or an effect so passing that the light flickers into only blacker night. And here—could there be any light at all?

It was a case—almost the only one possible— in which the mother has a right to stand between her child and ruin; to prevent her marrying a deliberate villain.

"Come to me, my darling," said she tenderly;

and drawing Adrienne to her lap, and shelter-
ing her there almost as in the days when,
long after babyhood, she would come and
"cuddle up" to her mother like a baby—Lady
de Bougainville explained, without any reserve,
as from perfect reliable sources she herself had
learnt it, what sort of life Mr. Summerhayes had
led : dissolute, unprincipled, selfish, mean—only
saved from the condign punishment that over-
takes smaller scoundrels by the exceeding charm
which still lingered about him, and would linger
to the last ; a handsome person, a brilliant intellect, and a frank fascination of manner, which
made the very people he was swindling and
cheating, ready to be cheated over again for the
mere pleasure of his society.

Such men exist—we all have known them ;
and those people who possess no very keen
moral sense often keep up acquaintance with
them for years ; in an easy surface way which,
they say, does no harm. But when it comes to
nearer ties—marriage for instance !—Mr. Summerhayes had once a mother, who was heard to

say, "If Owen ever marries a wife, God help her!"

"And," said Lady de Bougainville to herself, "God and *her* mother shall save my poor child from ever being his wife, if possible."

Still she was very just. She allowed, candidly, that only till Adrienne was twenty-one did her authority extend. "After that, my daughter, you may marry any one you please—even Mr. Summerhayes. But until then I will prevent you, even as I would prevent you from falling into the fire blindfold if I knew it. Do you understand? Have I wounded you very sore, my darling?"

Adrienne made no reply. She lay back with her head on Lady de Bougainville's shoulder, her face hidden from her. She neither sobbed nor wept, and offered not a single remonstrance or denial. At last, alarmed by her silence, Josephine lifted up the poor white face. It was blank: she had quietly fainted.

Lovers' agonies are sharp, and parents' cruelties many; but I think something might be said

on the other side. And, as anything suffered
for another is, in one sense, ten times harder
than anything one suffers for one's self, it seems
to me that the keenest of lovers' pain, the hot-
test of lovers' indignation, could hardly be
worse than the mingled grief and anger of that
poor mother, as she clasped her broken lily to
her breast, and hated, with a hatred as passionate as it was righteous, the man who had
brought such misery upon her little Adrienne.

As for Adrienne's father——But it was useless
to go to him, to ask him questions, or to exact
from him any promises. Nothing he said or did
could be in the smallest degree relied upon.
She must take the matter into her own hands,
and without delay.

It was Sunday morning, and the streets were
lying in that temporary quiescence when
religious Paris is gone to High Mass, and irre-
ligious Paris idling away its hours in early
deshabille, previous to blossoming out in *bour-
geois* splendour and gaiety. The Louvre
would be, as Mr. Summerhayes had probably

calculated, nearly empty ; an excellent trysting-place for lovers, or for mortal foes,—and her enemy, from first to last, this Owen Summerhayes had been. That he hated her too, Josephine had little doubt ; for she knew only too much of his career. But face him she would at once, before he could do her any more harm.

Leaving Adrienne in Bridget's charge—Bridget, who was only too quick to detect how matters stood, and might be trusted without one word too many—Lady de Bougainville, at the appointed hour, went to meet her daughter's lover.

Sir Edward was not with him : but Mr. Summerhayes had already come, and was pacing up and down the empty *salon*, inspecting the pictures more with the cool eye of an artist and connoisseur than the impatience of an expectant lover. In a moment, the quick womanly eye detected this fact, and in the indignant womanly heart the last drop of pity or sympathy was dried up for Mr. Summerhayes.

At sound of footsteps he turned round, with a well prepared and charming smile, and perceived Lady de Bougainville. It could not have been a pleasant meeting to him, man of the world as he was, and accustomed, no doubt, to a good many unpleasant things ; but externally it was civil enough. He bowed, she bowed, and then they stood facing one another.

They were nearly of an age, and they had personally almost equal advantages. Mentally, too ; except that probably the man had more brain than the woman—Lady de Bougainville possessing good common sense and general refinement, rather than intellect. In courage they were both on a par, and they knew it. The long warfare that had been waged between them, a sort of permanent fight over that poor weak soul, who was scarcely worth fighting for, had taught them their mutual strength and their mutual antipathy. Now the final contest was at hand.

"This is an unexpected pleasure, Lady de

Bougainville; I had no idea of meeting you here."

" No, you intended to meet my daughter; but instead, I thought I would come myself. There is nothing you can have to say to her which you cannot equally well say to her mother."

" Not exactly," returned Mr. Summerhayes. " To be plain with you, as I see you mean to be with me, my dear lady, you dislike me, and—I hope your daughter does not."

The smile on his lips made Josephine furious. As I have often said, she was not naturally a mild-tempered woman. It often cost her a great effort to restrain herself, as now.

" May I ask, Mr. Summerhayes, what grounds you have for supposing that Miss de Bougainville does not dislike you, or has the smallest feeling for you which could warrant your addressing to her such a letter as you sent her this morning?"

" You intercepted it, then ?"

" No, she gave it to me. She brought it to me at once, as she will bring every letter you

may choose to send her. My daughter and I
have always been on terms of entire confidence."

"Oh, indeed! A most happy state of
things!"

Nevertheless Mr. Summerhayes looked a little
disconcerted. Apparently his experience of
women had been of a different nature, and had
not extended to these bread-and-butter Misses,
whose extraordinary candour and trust in
their mothers produce such inconvenient results. But he was not easily nonplussed,
and in the present instance his necessities
were desperate, and admitted of no means
being left untried to attain his end. He advanced towards his adversary with a frank and
pleasant air.

"Mrs. Scanlan—I beg pardon, Lady de Bougainville, but we cannot readily forget, nor do
I wish to forget, old times—you do not like
me, I know, but you might at least be just to
me. You must perceive that I love your
daughter."

" Love !" she echoed contemptuously.

" Well, I wish to marry her—let us put it so, without discussing the rest. She was fond of me as a child, and I dare say she would be now. The difference of age between us is not so enormous. By the by, is it that you object to ?"

" No."

" Then what is it? My family? It is as good as her own. My fortune? That is small, certainly: but she is not poor. Myself personally? Well, such as I am you have known me these fifteen years, and whether you approve of me or not, your husband does. Let me remind you, Lady de Bougainville, that it is the father, not the mother, who disposes of a daughter's hand."

He was very cunning, this clever man; he knew exactly where to plant his arrows and lay his pitfalls; but for once a straightforward woman was more than a match for him.

" Adrienne cannot legally marry without her father's consent; but morally even his consent would not satisfy her without mine. And mine I never will give. You could not expect it."

" Why not ? It is an odd thing for a gentleman to have to ask, but no one likes to be condemned unheard. May I inquire, Lady de Bougainville, why 1 am so very objectionable as a son-in-law ? "

IIis daring was greater than she had anticipated, but somehow it only roused her own. The hackneyed simile of the lioness about to be robbed of her whelps was not inappropriate to Josephine's state of mind now. Every nerve was quivering, every feature tense with excitement. Her very fingers tingled with a frantic desire to seize the man by the throat, and shake the life out of him.

Despite his critical position, Mr. Summerhayes must have found her sufficiently interesting as an artistic study, to note down and remember ; for the year afterwards he exhibited in the Royal Academy a " Slaughter of the Innocents," in which the face of the half-mad mother was not unlike Lady de Bougainville.

This cold critical eye of his brought her to her senses at once.

"I will not have you for my son-in-law," she said in a slow, measured tone, "for a good many reasons, none of which you will much like to hear. But you shall hear them if you choose."

"Proceed, I am listening."

"First, you do not love my child; it is her money only you want. She is plain and not clever, not attractive in any way, only good; how could a man like you be supposed to love her? It is a thing incredible."

"Granted. Then take the other supposition, that I wish to marry her because she loves me."

"If she were so unfortunate as to do so, still she had better die than marry you. I say this deliberately, knowing what you are, and you know that I know it too."

"I am neither better nor worse than my neighbours," said he carelessly. "But come, pray inform me as to my own character. It may be useful information in case I should ever have the honour to call you mother-in-law."

Josephine went close up to his ear, almost whispering her words; nevertheless she said them distinct and sharp as sword cuts—the righteous sword which few women, and fewer men, ever dare to use. Perhaps the world would be better and purer if they did dare.

"You are a thief, because you cheat poor tradesmen by obtaining luxuries you cannot pay for; a swindler, because you borrow money from your friends on false pretences, and never return it; a liar, because you twist the truth in any way to obtain your ends. These are social offences. As for your moral ones"—Josephine stopped and blushed all over her matron face of forty years—but still she went on unshrinking. "Do you think I have not heard of poor Betsy Dale at the farm, and of Mrs. Hewson, your landlord's wife? And yet you dare to enter my doors and ask for *your* wife my innocent daughter! Shame upon you—seducer—adulterer!"

Bold man as he was, Mr. Summerhayes did look ashamed for a minute or so, but quickly recovered himself.

"This is strong language, somewhat unexpected from the lips of a lady; but I suppose necessary to be endured. In such a position what can a poor man do? I must let you have your own way—as I noticed in old times you generally had, Lady de Bougainville. Poor Sir Edward!"

The sneer, which she bore in silence, did not, however, prove sufficient safety-valve for his suppressed wrath, which was certainly not unnatural. He turned upon her in scarcely concealed fierceness.

"Still, may I ask, madam, what right you have thus to preach to me? Are you yourself so sublime in virtue, so superior to all human weaknesses, that you can afford to condemn the rest of the world?"

His words smote Josephine with a sudden humility, for she felt she had spoken strongly— more so, perhaps, than a woman ought to speak.

Besides, she had grown much humbler in many ways than she used to be.

"God knows," she said, "I am but too well aware of my own short-comings. But whatever I may be does not affect what you are. Nor does it alter the abstract right and wrong of the case; and no pity for you—I have been sorry for you sometimes—can blind my eyes to it. I must 'preach,' as you call it; I must testify against the wickedness of men like you so long as I am alive."

"Then you will be a—a rather courageous personage. In fact, a lady more instructive than agreeable. But let us come to the point," added he, casting off the faint gloss of politeness in which he had veiled his manner, and turning upon her a countenance which showed him a man fierce, unscrupulous, dangerous—controlled by nothing except the two grand restraints of self-interest and fear. "Lady de Bougainville, you know me and I know you. I also know your husband—perhaps a little too well; or he may have cause to think so. It is convenient for me to become his son-in-law, and to him to have me as such; for in the tender relations which would then exist between us I should hold my tongue. Otherwise, I shall not feel myself bound to do so. Therefore, you and I, I think, had better be friends than enemies."

It was possibly an empty threat; his last weapon in a losing fight. But in her uncertainty of the extent of his relations with her husband, in her total insecurity as to facts, Josephine felt startled for a moment. Only for a moment. If ever a woman lived in whom no compromise with evil was possible, it was Josephine de Bougainville. Sir Edward used to say, in old jocular days, that if his wife were to meet the devil in person, she might scorn him, or pity him, but she would certainly never be afraid of him. No more than she was now afraid of Mr. Summerhayes.

"You think to frighten me," she said, steadily; "but that is quite useless. I have already suffered as much as I can suffer. Do as you will—and I dare you to do it. I believe that

even in this world the right is always the strongest. You shall not marry my daughter! She
has been taught to love the right, and hate the
wrong. She will never love you. If you urge
her, or annoy her in any way, I will set the
police after you."

" You dare not."

" There is nothing I dare not do if it is to save
my child."

" And I suppose, to save your child, you will
go blackening me all over the world, crying out
from the housetops what a villain is Owen
Summerhayes."

" No, that is not my affair. I do not attack
you; I only resist you. If I saw a tiger roam-
ing about the forest, I should not interfere with
it; it may live its life, as tigers do. But if I
saw it about to spring upon my child, or any
other woman's child, I would take my pistol and
shoot it dead."

" As I verily believe you would shoot me,"
muttered Owen Summerhayes.

He looked at her, she looked at him. It was

in truth a battle hand to hand. Whether any
relic of conscience made the man fearful, as an
altogether clean conscience made the woman
brave, I cannot tell; but Mr. Summerhayes was
silent. They stood just under one of those
heavenly Madonnas of some old master—I know
not which—but they are all heavenly—is it not
always a bit of heaven upon earth, the sight of
a mother and child? Perhaps, vile as he was,
Summerhayes remembered his mother; or some
first love whom in his pure, early days he might
have made the happy mother of his lawful
child; possibly the angel which, they say, never
quite leaves the wickedest heart, stirred in his—
for he said respectfully, nay, almost humbly,
" Lady de Bougainville, what do you wish me
to do?"

She never hesitated a moment. Pity for him
was ruin to the rest.

" I wish you to quit Paris immediately, and
never attempt to see my daughter more."

" And if I dissent from this——"

Josephine paused, weighing well her words

—she had learnt to be very prudent now.

"I make no threats," she said; "I shall not speak, but act. My daughter is not yet eighteen; until twenty-one she is in my power. I shall watch her night and day. Any letter you write I shall intercept: but there is no need of that, she will give it to me at once. If you attempt an interview with her, I shall give you into the hands of the police. Besides this, no moral persuasion, no maternal influence, that I am possessed of, shall be spared to show you to her in your true colours, till she hates you—no, not you, but your sins—as I do now."

"You can hate, then?" And this clever man for a moment seemed to forget himself and his injuries in watching her; just as a curious intellectual study, no more.

"Yes, I can hate; Christian as I am, or am trying to be. God can hate too."

He laughed out loud. "I do not believe in a God;—do you? In your husband's God, for instance, who, as Burns neatly informs Him,

' Sends ane to heaven and ten to hell,
  A' for Thy glory,
And no for ony guid or ill
  They've done afore Thee.'"

Josephine answered the profanity of the man by dead silence. The great struggle of her inward life now, the effort to tear from heaven's truth its swaddling-clothes of human lies, was too sacred to be laid bare in the smallest degree before Owen Summerhayes.

"We have drifted away from our subject of conversation," she said at last; "indeed it has almost come to an end. You know my intentions—and me."

"I believe I have that honour: more honour than pleasure," he answered, with a satirical bow.

"You ought also to know, though I name it as a secondary fact, that it is upon me, and me alone, that my children are dependent; that I have power to make a will, and leave, or not leave, as I choose, every halfpenny of my fortune."

" Indeed," said Mr. Summerhayes, a little startled.

Lady de Bougainville smiled. "After this, in bidding you adieu, I have not the slightest fear but that our farewell will be a permanent one."

He bowed again, rather absently ; and then his eyes wandering round the room, lighted on two ladies watching him.

"Excuse me, but I see a friend; I have so many friends in Paris. Really it is quite *l'embarras de richesses*. May I take my leave of you, Lady de Bougainville ?"

Thus they parted : so hastily, that she hardly knew he was gone, till she saw him walking round the next *salon*, pointing out pictures to the two French ladies, one of whom, it was evident, admired the handsome Englishman extremely. As I question not, Mr. Summerhayes found many persons, both men and women, to admire him to the end of his days.

But that is neither here nor there. I have nothing to do with him, his course of life, or the circumstances of his latter end. Personally, he crossed no more, either for good or ill, the path of Lady de Bougainville.

When she had parted from him, she turned to walk homewards down the long cool galleries, now gradually filling with their usual Sunday stream of Parisian *bourgeoisie*, chattering merrily with one another, or occasionally stopping to stare with ignorant but well-pleased eyes at the Murillos, Titians, Raffaelles, which cover these Louvre walls. Josephine let it pass her by—the cheerful crowd, taking its innocent pleasure, "though," as some one said of a lark singing—"though it was Sunday." Then, creeping towards the darkest and quietest seat she could find, she sank there utterly exhausted. Her strength had suddenly collapsed, but it was no matter. The battle was done—and won.

CHAPTER XVIII.

A S I have said, the battle was ended : but
there followed the usual results of victory
—of ever so great a victory—picking up the
wounded and burying the slain.

Lady de Bougainville had only too much of
this melancholy work on hand for some days
following her interview with Mr. Summerhayes.
A few hours after her fainting-fit, Adrienne rose
from bed, and appeared in the household
circle just as usual, but for weeks her white
face was whiter, and her manner more listless
than ever. This love-fancy, begun in the merest
childhood, had taken deeper root in her heart
than even her mother was aware ; and the tear-
ing of it up tore some of the life away with
it.

She never blamed any one. "Mamma, you were quite right," she said, the only time the matter was referred to ; and then she implored it might never be spoken of again. "Mamma, dearest! I could not have married such a man ; I shall not even love him—not for very long. Pray be quite content about me."

But for all that, poor Adrienne grew weak and languid ; and the slender hold she ever had on life seemed to slacken day by day. She was always patient, always sweet, but she took very little interest in anything.

For Sir Edward, he seemed to have forgotten all about Mr. Summerhayes, and the whole affair of his daughter's projected marriage. He became entirely absorbed in his own feelings and sensations, imagining himself a victim to one ailment after another, till his wife never knew whether to smile or to feel serious anxiety. And that insidious disease which he really had —at least, I think he must have had, though nobody gave it a name—was beginning to show itself in lapses of memory so painful and so evidently involuntary, that no one ever laughed at them now, or said with sarcastic emphasis, "Papa forgets." Then, too, he had fits of irritability so extreme, mingled with corresponding depression and remorse, that even his wife did not know what to do with him. Nobody else ever attempted to do anything with him. He was thrown entirely upon her charge, and clung to her with a helpless dependence, engrossing her whole time and thoughts, and being jealous of her paying the slightest attention to any other than himself, even her own children. By this time they had quitted Paris, which he insisted upon doing, and settled temporarily in London : where, between him and Adrienne, who in his weakness, though not in his selfishness, so pathetically resembled her father, the wife and mother was completely absorbed—made into a perfect slave.

This annoyed extremely her son César, whose bright healthy youth had little pity for morbid fancies; and who, when he was told of the Summerhayes affair, considered his mother had

done quite right, and was furious at the thought
of his favourite sister wasting one sigh over
"that old humbug."

"I'll tell you what, mother—find Adrienne
something to do. Depend upon it, nothing
keeps people straight like having plenty to do.
Let us buy Brierley Hall, and then we will set
to work and pull it down and build it up again.
Fine amusement that will be—grand occupa-
tion for both Papa and Adrienne."

Lady de Bougainville laughed at her son's
rude boyish way of settling matters, but allowed that there was some common sense in the
plan he suggested. Only it annihilated, perhaps
for ever, her old dreams about Oldham Court.

"Oh, never mind that," reasoned the light-
hearted young fellow : "you shall go back
again some day. There are so many of us,
some will be sure to want Oldham Court to live
at; or you can have it yourself when we are all
married. It is securely ours ; Mr. Langhorne
tells me it is entailed on the family. Unless,
indeed, you should happen to outlive us all,

your six children and—say sixty grandchildren,
when you can sell it if you choose, and do what
you like with the money."

Laughing at such a ridiculous possibility,
Lady de Bougainville patted her son's head,
told him he was a great goose, but nevertheless
yielded to his reasoning.

In this scheme, when formally consulted—of
which formality he was now more tenacious
than ever—Sir Edward also condescended to
agree; and Adrienne, when told of it, broke into a faint smile at the thought of changing this
dreary hotel life for a real country home once more
—a beautiful old house with a park and a lake,
and a wood full of primroses and violets: for
Adrienne was a thorough country girl, who
would never be made into a town lady.

So Brierley Hall was bought, and the res-
torations begun, greatly to the interest of everybody, including the invalids, who brightened up
day by day. A furnished house was taken in
Brierley village, and thither the whole family removed: to be on the spot, they said, so as to

watch the progress of their new house, the rebuilding of which, César declared, was as exciting as the re-establishment of an empire.
True, this had not been done on the grand
scale which his youthful ambition planned, for
his wiser mother preferred leaving the fine old
exterior walls intact, and only remodelling the
interior of the mansion. But still it was an entirely new home, and in a new neighbourhood,
where not a soul knew anything of them, nor
did they know a single soul.

This fact had its advantages, as Josephine,
half pleasurably, half painfully, recognised. It
was a relief to her to dwell among strangers,
and in places to which was attached not one
sad memory—like that spot which some old
poet sings of, where

> "No sod in all the island green,
> Has opened for a grave."

"This is capital!" César would say, when he
and his mother took their confidential stroll
under the great elm avenue, or down the ivy

walk, after having spent hours in watching the proceedings of masons and carpenters, painters and paper-hangers. "I think rebuilding a house is as grand as founding a family—which I mean to do."

"Re-found it, as we are doing here," corrected his mother with a smile, for her son was growing out of her own conservative principles; he belonged to the new generation, and delighted in everything modern and fresh. They often had sharp merry battles together, in which she sometimes succumbed; as many a strong-minded mother will do to an eldest and favourite son, and rather enjoy her defeat.

César was very much at home this year, both because it was an interregnum between his college life and his choice of a profession, which still hung doubtful, and because his mother was glad to have him about her, supplying the need tacitly felt of "a man in the house,"—instead of a fidgety and vacillating hypochondriac. No one gave this name to Sir Edward, but all his family understood the facts of the case, and acted upon them. It was impossible to do otherwise. He was quite incapable of governing, and therefore was silently and respectfully deposed.

Nevertheless, by the strong influence of his ever-watchful guardian, his wife, the sacred veil of sickness was gradually dropped over all his imperfections; and though he was little consulted or allowed to be troubled with anything, his comfort was made the first law of the household, and everything done for the amusement and gratification of "poor papa." With which arrangement papa was quite satisfied, and, though he never did anything, doubtless considered himself as the central sun of the whole establishment: that is, if he ever thought about it at all, or about anything beyond himself. It was as difficult to draw the line where his selfishness ended and his real incapacity began, as it is in some men to decide what is madness and what actual badness. Some psychologists have started the comfortable but rather dangerous theory, that all badness must be madness. God knows!

Meantime, may He keep us all, or one day make us, sane and sound!

This condition of the nominal head of the household was a certain drawback when the neighbours began to call; and, as was natural, all the county opened its arms to Sir Edward and Lady de Bougainville and their charming family. For charming they were at once pronounced to be, and with reason. Though little was known of them beyond the obvious facts of a title, a fortune, and the tales whispered about by their servants of how they had just come from Paris, where they had mingled in aristocratic and even royal circles, still this was enough. And the sight of them, at church, and elsewhere, confirmed every favourable impression. They were soon invited out in all directions, and courted to an extent that even Sir Edward might have been content with, in the neighbourhood which they had selected as their future home.

But, strange to say, Sir Edward's thirst for society had now entirely ceased. He considered it an intolerable bore to be asked out to dinner; and when he did go, generally sat silent, or made himself as disagreeable as he had once been agreeable in company. The simple law of good manners—that a man may stay at home if he chooses, but if he does go out, he ought to make himself as pleasant as he can—was not recognised by poor Sir Edward. Nor would he have guests at his own house; it was too troublesome, he said, and he was sure nobody ever came to see him, but only to see the young people and their mother. He was not going to put himself out in order to entertain their visitors. So it came to pass, that in this large establishment the family were soon afraid of asking an accidental friend to dinner.

But over these and other vagaries of her master, which old Bridget used to tell me of, let me keep silence—the tender silence which Lady de Bougainville scrupulously kept whenever she referred to this period of her life, externally so rich, so prosperous, so happy. And, I believe, looked back upon from the distance of years, she herself felt it to have been so.

I think the same. I do not wish her to be
pitied overmuch, as if her life had been one
long tragedy; for that was not true: no lives
are. They are generally a mixture of tragedy
and comedy, ups and downs, risings and fall-
ings as upon sea-waves, or else a brief space of
sailing with the current over smooth sunshiny
waters, as just now this family were sailing. A
gay, happy, young family; for even Adrienne
began to lift up her head like a snow-drop after
frost, and go now and then to a dance or an archery meeting: while at the same time she was
steadily constant to the occupations she liked
best—walking, basket-laden, to the cottages
about Brierley, wherever there was anybody
sick, or poor, or old; teaching in the Sunday-
school; and being on the friendliest terms with
every child in the parish. Some of these, become grown-up fathers and mothers, had cherished, I found, such a tender recollection of her—
her mild, pale face, and her sweet ways—that
there are now in Brierley several little girls
called " Addy," or " Adorine," which was their

parents' corruption of the quaint foreign name
after which they had been christened, the name
of Miss de Bougainville.

Looking at her, her mother gradually became
content. There are worse things than an unfortunate love—a miserable marriage, for instance. And with plenty of money, plenty of
time, and a moderate amount of health (not
much, alas! for Adrienne's winter cough always
returned), an unmarried woman can fill up
many a small blank in others' lives, and, when
she dies, leave a wide blank for that hitherto
unnoticed life of her own.

They must, on the whole, have led a merry
existence, and been a goodly sight to see, these
young De Bougainvilles, during the two years
that Sir Edward was restoring Brierley Hall.
When they walked into church, filling the musty
old pew with a perfect gush of youth and
bloom, hearty boyhood and beautiful girlhood;
or when in a battalion, half horse, half foot,
they attended archery parties and cricket meetings, and pic-nics, creating quite a sensation,

and reviving all, the gaiety of the county—
their mother must have been exceedingly proud
of them.

"Only three of us at a time, please," she
would answer, in amused deprecation, to the
heaps of invitations which came for dinners, and
dances, and what not. "We shall overrun
you like the Goths and Vandals, we are so
many."

"We are so many!" Ah! poor fond mother,
planning room after room in her large house,
and sometimes fearing that Brierley Hall itself
would not be big enough to contain her children.
"So many!" Well, they are again the same
number now.

By the time the Hall was finished, the De
Bougainvilles had fairly established their position as one of the most attractive and popular
families in the neighbourhood. The young
people were pronounced delightful : the mother
in her beautiful middle-age was almost as young
as any of them, always ready to share in and
advance the amusements of her children, and

keep them from feeling their father's condition
as any cloud upon themselves. She stood a constant and safe barrier between him and them—a
steady wall, with sunshine on the one side and
shade on the other, but which never betrayed
the mystery of either. Many a time after a
sleepless night or a weary day she would quit
her husband for an hour or two, and come down
among her children with the brightest face possible, ready to hear of all their pleasures, share
in all their interests, and be courteous and cordial to their new friends; who, young and old,
were loud in admiration of Lady de Bougainville. Also, so well did she maintain his dignity, and shield his peculiarities by wise excuses,
that everybody was exceedingly civil, and even
sympathetic, to Sir Edward. He might have
enjoyed his once favourite amusement of dining
out every day, had he chosen; but he seldom
did choose, and shut himself up from society almost entirely.

At length the long deserted mansion was an
inhabited house once more. Light merry feet

ran up and down the noble staircase; voices, singing and calling, were heard in and out of the Hall; and every evening there was laughter, and chatter, and music without end in the tapestry-room, which the young De Bougainvilles preferred to any other. It was "so funny," they said; and when a house-warming was proposed, a grand ball, to requite the innumerable hospitalities the family had received since they came to the neighbourhood, César and Louis too—so far as Louis condescended to such mundane things, being a student and a youth of poetical mind—insisted that the dancing should take place there.

"It would be grand," said they, "to see these ghostly gentlemen and ladies looking down upon us flesh and blood creatures, so full of fun and enjoying life so much. Mamma, you must manage it for us. You can persuade papa to anything—persuade him to let us have a ball."

She promised, but doubtfully, and the question long hung in the balance, until some accidental caller happened to suggest to Sir Edward that with his rank and fortune he ought to take the lead in society, and give entertainments that would outshine the whole county. So one day he turned suddenly round, not only gave his consent to the ball, but desired that it might be given in the greatest splendour, and with no sparing of expense, so that the housewarming at Brierley Hall might be talked of for years in the neighbourhood. It was.

"Now, really, Papa has been very good in this matter," said César, rather remorsefully, to his sister, as they stood watching him creep from room to room, leaning on his wife's arm, and taking a momentary pleasure in the inspection of the preparations in the ball-room and supper-room. The young folks had now grown so used to their father's self-engrossed valetudinarianism that they took little notice of him, except to pay him all respect when he did appear among them, and get out of his way as soon as they could. As ever, he was the "wet blanket" upon all their gaiety—the cloud

in their sunshiny young lives.   But now he
could not help this ; once he could.

It was astonishing how little these young people saw of their father, especially after he came
to Brierley Hall. He had his own apartments, in
which he spent most of his time, rarely joining
the family circle except at meals.   His children's
company he never sought; they knew scarcely
anything of him and his ways, and their mother
was satisfied that it should be so.   The secrets
of the life to which she had once voluntarily
linked her own, and with which she had travelled on, easily or hardly, these many years,
were known to her, and her alone.   Best so.
Though she was constantly with him, and her
whole thought seemed to be to minister to his
comforts and contribute to his amusement, it
was curious how little she ever talked to her
children about their father.

The day of the ball arrived.   One or two
persons yet living, relics of the families then belonging to the neighbourhood, have told me of
it, and how splendid it was—finer than any en-

tertainment of the kind ever remembered about
Brierley. Though it was winter time, and the
snow lay thick upon the ground, people came
to it from fifteen miles round—the grand people
of the county. As for the poor people—Miss de
Bougainville's poor—they were taken by herself
beforehand to see the beautiful sight, the supper-room, glittering with crystal and plate, and
the decorated ball-room, which was really the
tapestry-room, both on account of César's wish,
and because Sir Edward thought, as a small
flight of stairs alone divided it from his bedroom, he would be able to go in and out and
watch the dancers, retiring when he pleased.
He had declined appearing at supper, which
would be far too much trouble; but he was gratified by the handsome appearance of everything, and in so bland a mood that he consented to his wife's desire that there should be next
day a second dance in the servants' hall, where
their humbler neighbours might enjoy the rem-
nants of the feast. And as she arranged all this
Lady de Bougainville felt in her heart that it

was good to be rich—good to have power in
her hands, so as to be able to make her children
and her friends happy—to spread for them a
merry, hospitable feast, and yet have enough
left to fill many a basket of fragments for the
poor.

"When your father and I are gone," she said
to César—after telling him what he was to do
as the young host of the evening—"when we
have slipped away and you reign here in our
stead, don't ever forget the poor: we were poor
ourselves once."

No one would have thought it who saw her
now, moving about her large house, and governing it with a wise liberality. All her petty, pathetic economies had long ceased: she dressed well,
kept her house well, and spared no reasonable
luxury to either herself or her children. She took
with pleasure in this, the first large hospitality she
had ever exercised—almost as much pleasure as
her children; until, just at the last moment, a
cloud was cast over their mirth by Sir Edward
taking offence at some trifle, becoming ex-

tremely irritable, and declaring he would not appear at night at all—they might manage things all themselves, and enjoy themselves without him, as they were in the habit of doing. And he shut himself, and his wife too, in his own room, whence she did not emerge till quite late in the day.

"It is very vexing, certainly," she owned to César, who was lying in wait for her as she came out; "but we must let him have his own way. Poor papa!"

And after her boy left her—for he was too angry to say much—Josephine stood for a minute or two at the window of the ante-room which divided her room from that of the girls, who were all dressing and laughing together. Once or twice she sighed, and looked out wistfully on the clear moonlight shining on the snow. Was she tired of this world, with all its vanities and vexations of spirit? Or was her soul, which had learnt much of late, full only of pity, and a certain remorseful sorrow that there should be nothing else but pity left, for the man

who had been her husband all these years? I
know not; I cannot sufficiently put myself in
her place to comprehend what her feelings must
have been. But whatever they were she kept
them to herself, and went with a smiling face
into her daughters' chambers.

There were two, one for the younger girls
—a quaint apartment, hung with Chinese
paper covered over with birds, and fishes, and
flowers; and another, the cheerfulest in the
house, where the firelight shone upon crimson
curtains and a pretty French bed, and left in
shadow the grim worn face of John the Baptist
over the fire-place; I know the room. There
Bridget stood brushing the lovely curls of Miss
Adrienne, for whom her mother had carefully
chosen a ball-dress, enveloping her defective
figure in clouds of white gauze, and putting
tender blush roses—real sweet-scented hothouse roses, in her bosom and her hair; so that
for once poor fragile Adrienne looked absolutely
pretty. For the two others, Gabrielle and Catherine, they looked pretty in anything. If I

remember right, Bridget told me they wore this night white muslin—the loveliest dress for any young girl—with red camellias in their bosoms, and I think ivy in their hair. Something real, I know it was, for their mother had a dislike to artificial flowers as ornaments.

She dressed, first her daughters and then herself; wearing her favourite black velvet, and looking the handsomest of them all. She walked round her beautiful rooms, glittering with wax lights, and tried to put on a cheerful countenance.

"It is a great pity of course, papa's taking this fancy; but we must frame some excuse for him, and not fret about it. Let us make ourselves and everybody about us as cheerful as we can."

"Yes, mamma," said Adrienne, whose slightly pensive but not unhappy face showed that, somehow or other, she too had already learnt that lesson.

"Mamma," cried César and Louis together, "you are a wonderful woman!"

Whether wonderful or not, she was the woman that God made her and meant her to be : nor had she wasted the gifts, such as they were. When, in years long after, her children's fond tongues being silent, others ventured to praise her, this was the only thing to which Lady de Bougainville would ever own. " I did my best," she would answer—her sweet, dim, old eyes growing dreamy, as if looking back calmly upon that long tract of time ; " Yes, I believe I did my best."

Most country balls are much alike ; so there is no need minutely to describe this one. Its most noticeable feature was the hostess and her children, who were, everybody agreed—and the circumstance was remembered for years—" quite a picture ;" so seldom was it that a lady, still young-looking enough to have passed for her eldest son's sister instead of his mother, should be surrounded by so goodly a family, descending, step by step, to the youngest child, with apparently not a single break or loss.

" You are a very fortunate and a very happy

woman," said to her one of her neighbours, who had lost much—husband, child, and worldly wealth.

"Thank God, yes!" answered gently Lady de Bougainville.

Everybody of course regretted Sir Edward's absence and his "indisposition," which was the reason assigned for it; though perhaps he was not so grievously missed as he would have liked to be. But everybody seemed wishful to cheer the hostess by double attentions; and congratulations on the admirable way in which her son César supplied his father's place. And, after supper, the Rector of Brierley, who was also the oldest inhabitant there, made a pretty little speech, giving the health of their absent host, and expressing the general satisfaction at Sir Edward's taking up his residence in the neighbourhood, and the hope that the De Bougainvilles of Brierley Hall might become an important family in the county for many generations.

After supper the young folks began dancing again, and the old folks looked on, sitting

round the room or standing round the doorway.
Lady de Bougainville looked on too, glancing
sometimes from the brilliantly-lighted crowd of
moving figures, to that other crowd of figures
on the tapestried wall, so silent and shadowy.
How lifelike was the one—how phantom-like
the other! Who would ever have thought
they would one day have changed places: those
all vanished, and these remained.

It was towards one o'clock in the morning
that a thing happened which made this ball an
event never forgotten in the neighbourhood
while the generation that was present survived.
Not only Bridget, but several extraneous spec-
tators, have described the scene to me as one
of the most startling and painful that it was
possible to witness.

The gaiety was at its climax: cheered by
their good supper, the dancers were dancing
and the musicians were playing their very best:
all but a few guests, courteously waited for by
César and Adrienne, had returned to the ball-
room; and Lady de Bougainville, supplying her

elder children's place, was moving brightly
hither and thither, smiling pleasantly on the
smiling crowd.

Suddenly a door was half opened—the door
at the further end leading by a short staircase
to Lady de Bougainville's bedchamber. Some
of the dancers shut it, but in a minute more it
was again stealthily set ajar, and a face peered
out—a weird white face, with long black hair
hanging from under a white tasselled night-
cap. It was followed by a figure, thin and
spare, wrapped in a white flannel dressing-
gown. The unstockinged feet were thrust into
slippers, and a cambric handkerchief strongly
perfumed was flourished in the sickly-looking
hands. Such an apparition, half sad, half ludi-
crous, was never before seen in a ball-room.

At first it was only perceived by those nearest the door, and they did not recognise it until
somebody whispered "Sir Edward." "He's
drunk, surely," was the next suggestion; and
one or two gentlemen spoke to him and tried to
lure him back out of the room.

No, he was not drunk; whatever his failings, intemperance had never been among them. It was something far worse, if worse be possible. The few who addressed him and met in return the vacant stare of that wild wandering eye, saw at once that it was an eye out of which the light of reason had departed, either temporarily or for ever.

The well-meant efforts to get him out of the room proved fruitless. He broke away with a look of terror from the hands which detained him, and began to dart in and out among the dancers like a hunted creature. Girls screamed —the quadrille was interrupted—the music stopped—and in the sudden lull of silence, Lady de Bougainville, standing talking at the further end of the room, heard a shrill voice calling her.

"Josephine! Josephine! Where is my wife? Somebody has taken away my wife!"

Whether she had in some dim way foreboded a similar catastrophe, and so when it came was partially prepared for it, or whether the vital necessity of the moment compelled her into almost miraculous self-control, I cannot tell; but the testimony of all who were present at that dreadful scene declares that Lady de Bougainville's conduct throughout it was something wonderful: even when, catching sight of her through the throng, the poor demented figure rushed up to her, and, as if flying there for refuge, clung with both arms about her neck.

"Josephine, save me! These people are hunting me down; I know they are. Dear wife, save me!"

She soothed him with quiet words, very quiet, though they came out of lips blanched dead-white. But she never lost her self-command for a moment. Taking no notice of anybody else—and indeed the guests instinctively shrunk back, leaving him and her together—she tried to draw her husband out of the room; but he violently resisted. Not until she said imperatively, "Edward, you *must* come," did he allow her to lead him, by slow degrees, through the ball-room to the door by which he had entered it.

It was a piteous sight—a dreadful sight.
There was not even the sublimity of madness
about it: no noble mind overthrown, no

"Sweet bells jangled out of tune and harsh;"

Sir Edward's condition was that of mere fatuity
—a weak soul sinking gradually into premature
senility. And the way in which his wife, so
far from being startled and paralysed by it,
seemed quite accustomed to his state, and un-
derstanding how to manage it, betrayed a
secret more terrible still, which had never before been suspected by her guests and good
neighbours. They all looked at one another
and then at her, with eyes of half-frightened
compassion, but not one of them attempted to
interfere.

She stood a minute—she, the tall, stately
woman, with her diamonds flashing and her
velvet gown trailing behind her, and that forlorn, tottering figure clinging to her arm—then,
casting a look of mute appeal to those nearest
her, whispered:

"Don't alarm my children, please. Take no

notice—let the dancing go on as before;" and was slipping out of sight with her husband, when Sir Edward suddenly stopped.

"Wait a minute, my dear," said he. A new whim seemed to strike him; he threw himself into an attitude, wrapping the folds of his dressing-gown about him something like a clergyman's gown, and flourishing his white pockethandkerchief with an air of elegant ease quite ghastly to witness.

"Ladies and gentlemen—no, I mean my dear friends and brethren—you see my wife, a lady I am exceedingly proud of; she comes of very high family, and has been the best and kindest friend to me." The sentence was begun *ore rotundo*, in a strained, oratorical, pulpit tone, gradually dwindling down almost to a whine.

"She is very kind to me still," he resumed, but querulously and petulantly, like a complaining child. "Only she worries me sometimes; she makes me eat my dinner when I don't want it; and, would you believe it?"—breaking into a silly kind of laugh—"she won't let me catch flies ! Not that there are many flies left to catch —it is winter now. I saw the snow lying on the ground, and I am so cold. Wrap me up, Josephine ; I am so very cold !"

Shivering, the poor creature clung to her once more, continuing his grumblings, which had dropped down to a mere mutter, quite unintelligible to those around. They shrunk away still further, with a mixture of awe and pity, whilst his wife half drew, half carried him up the few stairs that led to his bedroom-door. It closed upon the two ; and from that hour until the day when they were invited to his funeral, none of his neighbours, nor indeed any one out of his own immediate family, ever saw any more of poor Sir Edward de Bougainville.

And they heard very little either. The Brierley doctor, whom some one had sent for, came immediately, was admitted just as a matter of form, reported that the patient was asleep, but really seemed to know little or nothing about his illness. Nor did the sick man's own child-

ren, to whom everybody, of course, spoke delicately and with caution during the brief interval
that elapsed before the ball broke up and the
guests dispersed. They were very kindly and
considerate guests—would have done anything
in the world for their hostess and their family;
but the case seemed one in which nobody could
do anything. So, after a while, the last carriage
rolled away; César, left sole representative of
the hospitality of the family, saw the visitors
depart with due attention and many apologies,
but as few explanations as could possibly be
made. He was his mother's own son already,
both for reticence and self-control.

When the house was quiet, he insisted upon
all the servants and children going to bed; but
he and Adrienne, who had at first terribly broken down, and afterwards recovered herself,
spent the remainder of the night—the chilly
winter night—sitting on the little stair outside
their parents' door.

Once or twice the mother came out to them,
and insisted on their retiring to rest.

"Papa is fast asleep still—he may sleep till
morning—he often does. Indeed, I am quite
used to this, it never alarms me. Don't vex
your dear hearts about me, my children," she
added, breaking into a faint smile as she stooped over them and patted their hair. "You are
too young for sorrow. It will come in God's
own time to you all."

So said she, with a sigh; mourning over the
possible chance of her children's lives being as
hard as her own, nor knowing how vain was
the lamentation. Still, her feeling on this point
was so strong and immovable, that say what
they would, nothing could induce her to let
either son or daughter share her forlorn watch;
both then and afterwards she firmly resisted
all attempts of the kind. I fancy, besides the
reason she gave, there were others equally
strong—a pathetic kind of shame lest other
eyes than her own should see the wreck her
husband had become, and a wish to keep up to
the last, above all before her children, some
shadowy image of him in his best self, by which,

and not by the reality, he might be remembered after he was gone.

The end, however, was by no means at hand, and she knew it, or at least had good reason for believing so. The most painful thing about Sir Edward's illness was that the weaker his mind became, the stronger his body seemed to grow. Mr. Oldham's state had been pitiable enough, Josephine once thought, but here was the reasoning brain, not merely imprisoned, but slowly decaying within its bodily habitation, the mere physical qualities long outlasting— and God only knew how many years they might outlast—the mental ones; for Sir Edward was still in the middle of life. When she looked into futurity Josephine shivered; and horrible though the thought was to enter her mind, still it did enter, when he suffered very much,— that the heart-disease of which Dr. Waters had warned her, and against which she had ever since been constantly on her guard, might after all be less a terror than a mercy.

He did suffer very much at times, poor Sir

Edward! There were at intervals many fluctuations, in which he was pathetically conscious of
his own state, and to what it tended; nay, even
in a dim way, of the burthen he was, and was
likely to become to everybody. And he had an
exceeding fear of death and dying—a terror so
great that he could not bear the words spoken
in his presence. In his daily drives with his
wife—often with the carriage-blinds down, for
he could not endure the light, or the sight of
chance people—nothing would induce him to
pass Ditchley churchyard.

"It is very strange," Josephine would say to
Bridget, who now, as ever, either knew or
guessed more than any one her mistress's cares.
" He is so afraid of dying; when I feel so tired
—so tired!—when I would so gladly lay me
down to rest, if it were not for my children. ⌃
must try to live a little longer, if only for my
children."

But yet, Bridget told me, she saw day by day
Lady de Bougainville slowly altering under the
weight of her anxieties, growing wasted, and

old, and pale, with constant confinement to the one room, out of which Sir Edward would scarcely let her stir by night or by day. Seldom did she get an hour's refreshing talk with her children, who were entirely left to themselves in that large empty house, where of course no visitors were now possible. It would have been a dull house to them, with all its grandeur, had they not been, by all accounts, such remarkably bright young people, inheriting all the French liveliness and Irish versatility, based upon that solid groundwork of conscientiousness which their mother had implanted in them, implanted in her by the centuries' old motto of her race, " Fais ce que tu dois, advienne que pourra."

And so when that happened, which she must have long foreseen, and Sir Edward fell into this state, she and they still did the best they could, and especially for one another. The children kept the house cheerful ; the mother hid her heaviest cares within the boundary of that sad room. Oh, if rooms could tell their

history, what a tale to be told there! And
when she did cross its threshold, it was with a
steadfast, smiling countenance, ready to share
in any relaxation that her good children never
failed to have ready for her. And she took
care that all their studies and pursuits should
go on just the same, at home and at college,
except that César, who had no special call elsewhere, remained at Brierley Hall. She had
said to him one day, "I can't do without *you;*
don't leave me;" and her son had answered,
with his prompt decision, so like her own, "I
never will."

But as the summer advanced, and she felt
how dreary the young people's life was becoming, with that brave motherly heart of hers she
determined to send some of them away, out of
sight and hearing of her own monotonous and
hopeless days. For she had no hope; the best
physicians, who of course gave their best consideration to the case of so wealthy a man, and
so important a member of society (alas, the
mockery!) as Sir Edward de Bougainville, could

give her none. Cure was impossible; but the
slow decay might go on for many years. Nothing was left to her but endurance; the hardest possible lesson to Josephine de Bougainville.
She could fight with fate, even yet, but to stand
tamely with bound hands and feet, waiting for
the advancing tide, like the poor condemned
witches of old—it was a horrible trial. Yet
this was her lot, and she must bear it. In hers,
as in many another life, she needed to be taught
by means least expected or desired;—had to
accept the blessings which she never sought,
and lose those which she most prayed for : yet
long before the end came, she could say—I
have often heard her say—not " I have done
my best," but " He has done his best with me,
and I know it." And the *knowing* of it was the
lesson learned.

But just now it was very hard; and she felt
often, as she owned to Bridget, " tired—so
tired !" as if all the happiness that existence
could offer would not be equivalent to the one
blessing of rest.

I have said little about Bridget lately ; indeed
these latter years she had retired into what was
still called the nursery as a sort of amateur
young ladies' maid, occupying no very prominent position in the family. Her plain looks
had grown plainer with age ; Sir Edward disliked to see her about the house, and nothing
but his wife's strong will and his own weak one
could have retained in her place the follower of
the family. In the sunshine of prosperity poor
Bridget retired into the shade, but whenever a
cloud came over the family, her warm Irish
heart leaped up to comfort them all ; her passionate Irish fidelity kept their secrets from
every eye ; and her large Irish generosity forgot
any little neglect of the past, and flung itself
with entire self-devotion into the present. (This
little ebullition must be pardoned. I was very
fond of Bridget, who stood to me as the type
of all that is noble in the Irish character, which
is very noble at its core.)

During this sad summer Bridget rose to the
emergencies of the time. She lightened her

mistress's hands as much as possible, becoming
a sort of housekeeper, and doing her duties
very cleverly, even in so large an establishment
as Brierley Hall. For there was no one else to
do it; Adrienne was not able; it was as much
as Bridget's caution could do to conceal from
her mistress a care which would have added
heavily to all her other burthens, namely, that
things were not quite right with poor Miss Adrienne. Her winter cough lingered still. That
gay ball-dress in which she had looked so
pretty, proved a fatal splendour; during the
long chilly night when she and César had sat
at their mother's room door, the cold had
pierced in through her bare neck and arms. She
scarcely felt it; her mind was full of other things;
and when, in the grey dawn, she took out of
her bosom the dead hothouse roses gathered by
her mother with such care, she little thought,
nor did anyone think, that underneath them
Death himself had crept in and struck her to
the heart.

Not a creature suspected this. That strange

blindness which sometimes possesses a family which for many years has known neither dangerous sickness nor death, hung over even the mother. She was so accustomed to Adrienne's delicacy of health, and to Bridget's invariable cheery comment upon it, " It's the cracked pitcher goes longest to the well," that her eyes detected no great change in the girl. And Adrienne herself said nothing ; she was so used to feeling " a little ill," that she took her feebleness quite as a matter of course, and only wished to make it as little of a trouble as possible—above all to her mother, who had so many cares ; and she urged with unselfish earnestness a plan Lady de Bougainville arranged, and at last brought about, that the three boys should go with an Oxford tutor on a reading-party to Switzerland for two months.

César resisted it a long time. " I will not leave you, mother. You said I never must."

" I know that, my son, and I want you very much, but I shall want you more by-and-by. This kind of life may last for years—years ! I can bear it better when I see my children happy. Besides," added she more lightly, "I could not trust your brothers without you—you grave old fellow! You are the stronghold of the house. Nevertheless, you must do as your mother bids you a little while longer. Obey her now, my darling, and go." So César went.

The morning of departure was sunshiny and bright, and the three lads were bright as the day. It was natural—they were so gay, and healthy, and young : their sisters too—to whom they promised heaps of things to be brought home from Switzerland. Adrienne was the only one who wept. She, clinging to César, always her favourite brother, implored him to "take care of himself," and be sure to come home at the two months' end.

"Ay, that I will! Nothing in the world shall stop me for a day," cried he, shaking his long curls—very long hair was the fashion then —and looking like a young fellow bound to conquer fate, and claim from fortune everything he desired.

" Very well," said his mother, gaily. " Come back on the first of October and you'll find us all standing here, just as you leave us. Now be off! Good-bye—good-bye."

She forced the lads away, with the laugh on her lips and the tears in her eyes. Yet she was not sad—glad rather, to have driven her children safe out of the gloomy atmosphere which she herself had to dwell in, but which could not fail to injure them more or less.

" The young should be happy," she said, half-sighing; " and, bless them! these boys will be very happy. What a carriage-full of hope it is !"

She watched it drive away, amidst a grand farewell waving of hats and handkerchiefs, and then turned back with her three daughters into the shadows of the quiet house, gulping down a wild spasm at her throat, but still content— quite content. Women that are mothers will understand it all.

CHAPTER XIX.

IN this straightforward telling of the history of my dear Lady de Bougainville, I pause, almost with apprehension. I am passing out of the sunshiny day, or the chequered lights and glooms which, viewed from a distance, seem like sunshine, into the dark night—as she had now to pass. The events next to be recorded happened so suddenly, and in such rapid succession, that in the recording of them they seem a mountain of grief too huge for fate to heap at once upon one individual. Yet is it not true to the experience of daily life that sorrows mostly come 'in battalions?'"

Lady de Bougainville had had many perplexities, many trials, many sore afflictions; but one solemn Angel had always passed by her door without setting his foot there, or taking any treasures thence, except indeed her little new-born babies. Now, on that glorious August day, he stood behind her, hiding his bright still face with his black wings, on the very threshold of Brierley Hall.

After the boys had departed, Bridget came to her mistress, and hastily, with fewer words than voluble Bridget was wont to use, asked if she might go up to London with the young ladies and their governess for some little pleasuring that had been planned.

"And I'm thinking, my lady, if afterwards I might just take Miss Adrienne to see the doctor" (a physician of note who sometimes attended the family). "She's growing thin, and losing her appetite of late: fretting a little, maybe, at losing her brothers. But now they're fairly gone, she'll soon get over it."

"Of course she will," said the mother, smiling; for Bridget spoke so carelessly that even she was deceived. Doubly deceived next day by her daughter's red cheeks and sparkling eyes, caused by the excitement of this brief two-hours' journey.

"You don't look as if you needed any doctor, my child. However, you may go, just to satisfy Bridget. Mind and tell me all he says to you."

But when they came back there was nothing to tell; at least Adrienne reported so: "All the doctor's orders were given to Bridget in the next room; he only patted me on the shoulder, and bade me go home and get strong as fast as ever I could—which I mean to do, Mamma; it would be such a trouble to you if I were ill. There's papa calling you! run back to him—quick—quick!"

It happened to be one of Sir Edward's bad days, and not till quite late at night had his constant nurse—for he would have no other—a chance of leaving him and creeping down-stairs for a little rest in the cedar parlour. There she found Bridget waiting for her, as was her frequent habit, with a cup of tea, after all the rest of the household was in bed.

"Thank you!" Josephine had said, and no more—for she had no need to keep up a smiling face before her faithful old servant—and she was utterly worn out with the long strain of the day.

Bridget once told me that as she stood beside her mistress that night, and watched her take that cup of tea, she felt as if it were a cup of poison which she herself had poured out for her drinking.

"Now," continued Lady de Bougainville, a little refreshed, "tell me, for I have just ten minutes to spare, what the doctor said about Miss Adrienne. Nothing much, it seems, except telling her to go home and get strong. She will be quite strong soon, then?"

The question was put as if it scarcely needed an affirmative, and Bridget long remembered her mistress's look, and even her attitude, sitting comfortably at ease with her feet on the fender and her gown a little lifted, displaying her dainty silk stockings and black velvet shoes.

"Why don't you answer?" asked she, sudden-

ly looking up. " There is nothing really wrong
with the child?"

" There is—a little"—said Bridget, cautiously.
" I've thought so, my lady, a good while, only I
didn't like to tell you. But the doctor said I
must. He is coming down to-morrow to speak
to you himself."

" To speak to me !"

" It's her lungs, you see ; she caught cold in
winter, and has coughed ever since. He wants
to bring a second doctor down to examine her
chest, and I thought you might be frightened,
and that I had better——"

Frightened was not the word. In the mother's face was not terror, but a sort of instan-
taneous stony despair, as if she accepted all and
was surprised at nothing. Then it suddenly
changed into fierce, incredulous resistance.

" I abhor doctors. I will not have these men
coming down here and meddling with my
child : she should never have gone to town.
You take too much upon yourself, Bridget,
sometimes."

Bridget never answered; the tears were rolling fast down her cheeks, and the sight of them seemed to alarm Lady de Bougainville more than any words.

She held out her hand. "I did not mean to be cross with you. I know I am very cross sometimes, but I have much to bear. Oh, if anything were to go wrong with my child! But tell me—tell me the whole truth; it is best."

Bridget knew it was best, for the doctor would tell it all, in any case, to-morrow; and his opinion, as expressed to herself, had been so decided as to leave scarcely a loophole of hope. It was the common tale—a neglected cold, which, seizing upon Adrienne's feeble constitution, had ended in consumption so rapid that no remedies were possible: indeed the physician suggested none. To the patient herself he had betrayed nothing, of course, sending her away with that light cheery speech; but to the nurse he had given distinctly and decisively the fiat of doom. Within a few months, perhaps even a few weeks, the tender young life would be ended.

The whole thing was so sudden, so terrible, that even Bridget herself, who had had some hours to grow familiar with it, scarcely believed the words she felt herself bound to speak. No wonder, therefore, that the mother was utterly and fiercely incredulous.

"It is not true! I know it is not true!" she said. "Still something must be done. I will take her abroad at once—ah, no! I can't do that—but you will take her, Bridget. She shall go anywhere—do anything—thank God we are so rich!"

"If the riches could save her, poor darling!" broke in Bridget, with a sob. "I never told you how ill she was; she would not let me; she said you had enough to bear. But when you see how much she suffers daily, and may have to suffer, the doctor says—oh, my lady!—you will let the child go."

"I will not!" was the fierce cry. "Anything but this; oh, anything but this!"

M 2

Josephine had known many sorrows—almost
every kind of sorrow except death. True, she
had mourned over her lost babies, and for her
father; though his decease, happening peacefully at a ripe old age and soon after her own
marriage, was scarcely felt at the time as a real
loss. But that supreme anguish which sooner
or later smites us all, when some one well-be-
loved goes from us, never to return—leaving behind a deep heart-wound, which closes and heals
over in time, yet with a scar in its place for
ever—this Josephine had never known nor understood till now.

Nor did she now—even though, after the
doctors had been, the truth was forced upon her
from the lips of her own child.

"Mamma," whispered Adrienne, one day,
when, in the pauses of sharp suffering which
often troubled a decay that otherwise would
have been as beautiful as that of an autumn
leaf, she lay watching her two sisters amusing
themselves in the room, from which she seldom
stirred now, "Chère maman, I think after all

Gabrielle will make the best Miss de Bougainville. Hush!" laying her hand on her mother's
lips, and then reaching up to kiss them, they
had turned so white; "I know all; for I asked
Bridget, and she told me. And I am not afraid.
You may see I am not afraid."

She was not. Either from her long-confirm-
ed ill-health, and perhaps her early disappointment, life had not been so precious to poor little
Adrienne as they had thought it was; or else,
in that wonderful way in which dying people,
though ever so young, grow reconciled to dying,
death had ceased to have any terrors for her.
Her simple soul looked forward to "heaven,"
and the new existence there, with the literal
faith and confidence of a child; and she talked
of her own departure, of where she would like
to be buried, and of the flowers that were to be
planted over her—" that I may spring up again
as daisies and primroses: I was so fond of
primroses "—with a composure that sometimes
was startling to hear.

"You see, Bridget," she would say, "after I

am gone, mamma will not be left forlorn, as if I were her only one. She will still have two daughters, both much cleverer and prettier than I, and her three sons—oh, such sons !—to carry down the name to distant generations. I can be the easiest spared of us all."

And in her utter unselfishness, which had been Adrienne's characteristic from birth, she would not have her brothers sent for, or even told of her state, lest it might shorten their enjoyments abroad, and bring them sooner back to a dreary home.

" I can love them all the same," she said, " and I want them to remember me with love, and not in any painful manner. If they just come in time for me to say good-bye to them—I should like that—it will do quite well."

Thus, in the quietest and most matter-of-fact way, her sole thought being how she could give least trouble to anybody, Adrienne prepared for her solemn change.

Was her mother also prepared? I cannot tell. Sometimes Bridget thought she seemed to

realize it perfectly, and was driven half frantic
by the difficulty she had in getting away from
her husband—who remained much in the same
state—to her poor child, with whom every
moment spent was so precious. Then again,
as if in total blindness of the future, she would
begin planning as usual her girls' winter dresses
—her *three* girls; or arranging with eagerness,
long beforehand, all the Christmas festivities
and Christmas charities which Adrienne was to
give to her poor people, who came in dozens to
ask after Miss de Bougainville, and brought her
little offerings of all sorts without end.

"See what a blessing it is to be rich!" Lady
de Bougainville would say. "When I was at
Ditchley I used to dread Christmas, because we
were so poor we could do nothing for anybody: now we can. How we shall enjoy it
all!"

Adrienne never contradicted her, and entered
into her arrangements as if she herself were
certain to share them; but sometimes, when
Lady de Bougainville had quitted the room,

she would look after her with a sigh, saying, "Poor mamma! poor mamma!"

Yet it would be a mistake to suppose that Adrienne's illness was altogether a miserable time. I think mere sickness—nay, mere death—never is, unless the poor sufferer helps to make it so. By degrees the whole household caught the reflection of Adrienne's wonderful peace and contentment in dying. The leaves that she watched falling, and the flowers fading—it happened to be a remarkably beautiful autumn—did not fall and fade in a more sunshiny calm than she.

"I know I shall never 'get up May hill,' as Bridget expresses it, but I may have a few months longer among you all. I should like it; if I didn't trouble you so very much."

By which she meant her own sufferings, which were often very severe—more so than any one knew, except Bridget. The nurse with her child, the wife with her husband, throughout all that dreary time, shared and yet concealed one another's cares; and managed somehow to keep

cheery, more or less, for the sake of Gabrielle
and Catherine, who were now the only bit of
sunshine left in Brierley Hall. It began to feel
chill and empty; and every one longed for, yet
dreaded, the boys' return, when one day, after
the bright autumn had turned almost to premature winter, Adrienne drew her mother's face
down to hers, over which had come a great and
sudden change, and whispered, "Write to my
brothers: tell them to come home."

So Lady de Bougainville wrote a letter in
which for the first time she broke to her sons
something of the truth, and why, by Adrienne's
desire, it had been hitherto concealed from
them.

"Come home quick," she wrote—(I have myself read the letter, for it was returned to her,
and found years after among her other papers).
"Come, my sons, though your merry days are
done, and you are coming home to sorrow.
You have never known it before; now you
must. Your mother cannot save you from it
any longer. Come home, for I want you to

help me. My heart is breaking. I sometimes
feel as if I could not live another day, but for
the comfort I look forward to in my three dear
boys."

Thus wrote she, thus thought she at the
time. Years after, how strange it was to read
those words!

The letter sent, Adrienne seemed to revive a
little. It was the middle of September. " They
will be home, you'll see, on the first of October;
César never breaks his word. He will not find
me on the hall-door steps as you promised him,
mamma; but he *will* find me, I feel sure of
that; I shall just see them all—and then——"
Then?

That night, when forced to quit her daughter's cheerful side to keep watch in the gloomy
bedroom which Sir Edward had insisted upon
furnishing so sumptuously, with a huge cata-
falque of a bed to sleep in, and tall mirrors to
reflect his figure, the miserable little stooping
figure!—that night, and in that chamber, where
the blessedness of married solitude had become

a misery untold, Lady de Bougainville for the
first time in her life meditated solemnly upon
the other world, whither—in how few days or
hours, who could tell?—Adrienne was so fearlessly going.

It might have been that in the cloud which had
fallen upon so many of her mortal delights, the
blankness that she found in her worldly splen-
dours, Josephine's mind had grown gradually prepared for what was coming upon her; or perhaps
on that special day—she had reason to remember
it—the invisible world was actually nearer to
her than she knew; but she sat by her fire long
after her husband was asleep—sat thinking and
thinking, until there seemed to be more than
herself in the room, and the portraits of her
children on the walls followed her wistfully
about, as the eyes of portraits do. She grew
strangely composed, even though she knew her
daughter was dying. We never recognise how
we have been taught these kind of things, nor
who is teaching us, but to those who believe in
a spiritual world at all, there come many in-

fluences totally unaccounted for : we may have
learnt our lesson unawares, but we have learnt
it, and when the time comes we are ready.

It was one of the latter days of September
—I think the 29th—that the *Times* newspaper
communicated to all England, in a short paragraph, one of those small tragedies in real life
which sometimes affect us outsiders more than
any wholesale catastrophe, shipwreck, earth-
quake, or the like. The agony is so condensed
that it seems greater, and comes more closely
home to us. We begin to think how we should
feel if it happened to ourselves, and how those
feel to whom it has happened, so that our hearts
are full of pity and sympathy.

Thus, on that 29th September many a worthy
father of a family, enjoying his *Times* and his
breakfast together, stopped to exclaim " How
shocking !" and to read aloud to wife or
children, mingled with sage reflections on the
dangers of Alpine exploits and of foreign travelling in general, the account of an accident
which had lately befallen some Swiss tourists,

in crossing the Lake of Uri from Bauen to Tell's chapel. They had put up a small sail in their crowded boat, and one of the sudden squalls which, coming down from the mountains all round it, render this one of the most perilous of the Swiss lakes, had caught and capsized them. Two of their number, said to be English—Oxford men, named Bourgoyne—were drowned.

Lower down, inserted as "from a Correspondent," was another version of the catastrophe; explaining that the number in the boat was only five; three young men; an elderly gentleman, their tutor; and the boatman. The two latter had saved themselves by swimming, and were picked up not far from Bauen; but the three young fellows, brothers, after making ineffectual attempts to help one another, had all gone down. They were sons of an English gentleman of fortune, this account said; and their names were not Burgoyne, but De Bougainville.

Twenty-five years ago there was no electric

telegraph, and a very uncertain foreign post; the *Times'* couriers often outsped it, and news appeared there before any private intelligence was possible. Thus it happened that she of whom many a kind-hearted English matron thought compassionately that morning, wondering if those three poor lads had a mother how the news was broken to her, and how she bore it,—had no warning of the dreadful tidings at all. She read them—read them with her own eyes, in the columns of the *Times* newspaper!

Sir Edward's sole remaining interest in the outside world was his daily paper. How much of it his enfeebled mind took in was doubtful, but he liked to hear it read to him in his wife's pleasant monotonous voice; while to her this was rather a relief than not, for it killed two hours of the long dreary day. Besides, she got into a habit of reading on and on, without comprehending a single sentence: nay, often thinking of something else the whole time. As she did this morning: wondering if her boys had reached Calais, and what sort of a crossing they would have, for the wind had been howling all night in the chimneys of Brierley Hall. Not that she was afraid of the sea, or indeed of anything: none of those sudden misfortunes which are the portion of some lives had ever happened in hers. Though she had had no answer to her letter, it never occurred to her to be uneasy about her sons. They were sure to come home again, and in good health, for, except Adrienne, all her children inherited her own excellent constitution. That very morning she had said to Bridget, half sadly, " Oh yes. I am quite well —always am well. I think nothing could ever kill me."

She had just finished the leading articles and was turning to the police reports—anything did for reading—when this fatal paragraph caught her eye. It might not have done so, so preoccupied was she, but for the word " Switzerland," which reminded her of her boys. So she paused to glance over it, first to herself; read it once —twice—thrice—before she could in the least take it in. When she did, her strong soul and

body alike gave way. She threw up her arms
with a wild shriek, and fell flat on the floor like
a stone.

Admission to Sir Edward's room was rare.
Sometimes whole days passed without the
younger girls being sent for even to say good-
morning or good-night to papa—all they ever
did; and it was weeks since Adrienne had seen
her father. He made no inquiry after her;
seemed scarcely aware of her state, except to
grudge her mother's absence in her room. Thus,
after the morning visit to her sick child, it was
so usual for Lady de Bougainville to spend the
whole forenoon shut up with her husband, that
nobody inquired for her, or thought of inquiring,
until Bridget, noticing that among the letters
which came in by the post was a foreign one,
and not in any of the boys' handwriting,
thought she would take it in to her mistress herself, and so bring sooner to Miss Adrienne, who
was very feeble that day, the news of her brothers' arrival, and the hour.

Bridget knocked several times, but no one

answered. Then, terribly alarmed, she pushed open the double doors of green baize, which shut off all sounds in that room from the rest of the house, and ventured in. There, the sight she saw almost confirmed a dreadful possibility which she had never dared to breathe to mortal, but which haunted poor Bridget night and day.

Sir Edward sat with his wife's head upon his knees; she lying as if she were dead,—killed, in fact;—and he stroking, with a miserable sort of moan, her hands and her hair.

"Come here, Bridget; tell me what is the matter with her! I haven't hurt her, indeed I have not. I never even said one unkind word. She was just quietly reading the newspaper, when down she dropped as if somebody had shot her. Is she dead, I wonder? Then people will be sure to say I killed her. Take her, Bridget, for I must run and hide."

He shifted the poor head from his own lap to Bridget's, and the movement brought a sigh of returning life to the breast of the unfortunate mother.

Josephine had said to her eldest son in the letter which never reached him, for it came back to her unopened, that "her heart was breaking." But hers was not one of the hearts that break.

She opened her eyes, lifted herself up on her elbow, and stared wildly round.

"Something has happened. Is it Adrienne?" And then she caught sight of the newspaper on the floor. "Ah, no! It is my boys!" she shrieked. "Bridget, my boys are dead—drowned in the lake!—the newspaper says so."

"Newspapers don't always tell the truth," cried Bridget; and, terrified and bewildered as she was, bethought herself of the letter in her hand. Together the two women managed to break it open and read it, spelling it out with horrible exactness, word by word.

Alas, no! There was no refutation, nor even modification of the truth. In mercy, perhaps, came the speedy confirmation of it, before any maddening gleam of hope could arise. Her three sons were all dead—drowned and dead.

Before this letter of the tutor's was written, the
" bodies"—ghastly word!—had been recovered
from the lake, identified, and buried; half the
population of Bauen, and all the English
strangers for many miles round, following them
to the grave. The three brothers slept side by
side in a little out-of-the-way Swiss churchyard,
and the name of De Bougainville was ended.

. To realize the blow in all its extent was impossible. Josephine did not, or her reason
would have left her. As it was, for an hour or
more poor Bridget thought she had gone quite
insane. She did not faint or in any way lose
her consciousness again, but kept walking up
and down the room, rapidly calling upon her
sons by name one after the other, then falling
on her knees and calling upon God.

It was an awful agony; the more so as, except
by her poor servant, who watched her terrified,
but attempted no consolation, it was an agony
necessarily unshared. Sir Edward had crept
away into a corner, muttering, " Josephine, be
quiet—pray be quiet;" and then relapsing into

his customary childish moan. At first she took
no notice of him whatever; then, catching sight
of him, with a sudden impulse, or perhaps a
vague hope of giving or getting consolation,
she went up to him, put her arms about his neck
and laid her head on his shoulder.

"Edward, dear husband," she cried in a wail-
ing voice, "Edward, our sons are dead! Do
you understand? Dead—all dead. You will
never see one of them any more."

He patted her cheek, and kissed her with his
vacant smile. "There now, I knew you'd soon
be quiet. And don't cry, Josephine; I can't
bear to see you cry. What were you saying
about the boys? Dead? Oh, nonsense! They
were to be home to-night. Bridget, just ring
the bell, and ask one of the servants if the young
gentlemen are come home."

Josephine rose up, unlocked her arms from
her husband's neck, and stood looking at him a
minute. Then she turned away, and walking
steadily to the middle of the room, stood there
again, for ever so long; dumb and passive as a

rock; with all her waves of misery breaking
over her.

"My lady," said Bridget, at length venturing
to touch her.

"Well?"

"I must go. I dare not leave Miss Adrienne
any longer."

"Adrienne, did you say?" And the mother's
heart suddenly turned—as perhaps Bridget had
meant it should turn—from her dead sons to
her still living daughter.

"Miss Adrienne is sinking fast, I think."

"Sinking! that means dying."

Lady de Bougainville said the word as if it
had been quite familiar, long-expected, painless.
Hearing it, Bridget wondered if her mistress's
mind were not astray again, but she looked
"rational like," and even smiled as she clasped
her faithful servant's hand.

"Do not be afraid, Bridget; I am quite myself now. And I have been thinking—Adrienne
was so fond of her brothers. I don't know
where they are,"—and the wild, bewildered

stare came into her eyes again,—"but I suppose, wherever they are, she will go to them;
and soon, very soon. Why need we tell her
of their death at all?"

"My lady, you could not bear it," cried
Bridget, bursting into tears. "To go in and out
of her room all day and all to-morrow—for she
says she *will* stay till the day after to-morrow
—and hear her talk so beautifully about you
and them, you could not bear it."

"I think I could, if it were easier for my
child. Let us try."

Without another word Josephine went and
washed her face, combed out her long grey
hair, which had fallen down dishevelled from
under her cap, arranged her collar and brooch,
and then came and stood before Bridget with a
stedfast, almost smiling countenance.

"Look at me now. Would she think anything was wrong with me?"

"No, no," sobbed Bridget, choking down
her full Irish heart, half bursting with its impulsive grief. But when she looked at her mis-

tress she could not weep; she felt ashamed.

Lady de Bougainville took her old servant's hand. "You can trust me, and I can trust you. Go in first, Bridget, and tell my child her mother is coming."

And, a few minutes after, the mother came. All that long day, and the next, she went about her dying child—moving in and out between Adrienne's room and her husband's—(for Sir Edward had taken to his bed, declaring he was "very ill," and kept sending for her every ten minutes)—but never by word or look did she betray the calamity which had fallen upon her, and upon the household.

Adrienne said often during that time, "Mamma, I am such a trouble to you!" but no; her brief young life remained a blessing to the last. While the rest of the house was shut up, and the servants moved about noiselessly with frightened faces, awed by the sorrow which had fallen upon the family—within Adrienne's room all was peace. While every other room was darkened, there her mother would not have

the blinds drawn down, and the soft yellow
sunshine fell cheerfully across the bed, where,
quiet as a baby and almost as pretty, in her
frilled night-gown and close cap, she slept that
exhausted sleep—the forerunner of a deeper
slumber, of which she was equally unafraid.

Nothing seemed to trouble her now. Once
only she referred to her brothers. "Mamma,
there are twenty-four hours still,"—to the first
of October she evidently meant. "I may not
stay with you so long."

"Never mind, my darling."

"No, I do not mind—not much. You will
give my love to the boys; and tell them to be
good to you, and to Gabrielle and Catherine. They will: they were always such good
boys."

"Always—always!"

Here Bridget came forward, and suggested
that the mother had better go and lie down for
a little.

"No; let her go to bed properly: she looks
so tired. Good night, mamma," and Adrienne

held up her face to be kissed. " You will come to me the first thing to-morrow morning."

" Yes, my child."

She tottered out, and between her daughter's room and her husband's Josephine dropped insensible on the floor—where Bridget found her some minutes afterwards. But nobody else knew.

To Adrienne the morning and the mother's morning kiss never came. In the middle of the night, Bridget, who lay by her side asleep— " sleeping for sorrow," woke, with a feeble touch trying to rouse her.

" I feel so strange, Bridget. I wonder what it is. Is it dying ? No, no," (as Bridget started up;) " don't go and wake mamma—at least, not yet. She was so very tired."

The mother was not wakened; for in a few minutes more, before Bridget dared to stir—with her head on her nurse's shoulder and her hand holding hers, like a little child, Adrienne died.

*   *   *   *   *   *   *

As I said a while ago, I hardly know how to
make credible the events which followed so rapidly after one another, making Brierley Hall
within the six months an empty, desolate,
childless house. And yet they all happened
quite naturally, and by a regular chain of circumstances—such as sometimes befalls, in the
most striking way, a family from which death
has been long absent, or has never entered at
all.

At the time of Adrienne's illness there was
raging in Brierley village a virulent form of
scarlet fever. Lady de Bougainville had not
heard of this; or if she had, her own afflictions
made her not heed it. When, before the funeral,
a number of Miss de Bougainville's poor—children and parents too—begged permission to look
once more at her sweet face as it lay in the
coffin, the mother consented, and even gave
orders that these, her child's friends, should be
taken in and fed and comforted, though it was
a house of mourning. And so it happened that
the death they came to see they left behind

them. The fever, just fading out of the' cottages, took firm hold at the Hall. First a servant sickened; a girl who waited on the young ladies, and then the two children themselves. The disease was of the most malignant and rapid form. Almost before their mother was aware of their danger, both Gabrielle and Catherine had followed their brothers and sisters to the unknown land. They died within a few hours of one another, and were buried on the same day.

"How can you live?" said Dr. Waters and Mr. Langhorne, coming back from the funeral, where, the father being incapable, they had acted as chief mourners. "How will you ever live?" And the two old men wept like children.

"I must live," answered Josephine, without the shadow of a tear upon her impassive, immoveable face: "look at him!" She pointed to her husband, who stood at the window, absorbed in his favourite amusement of catching flies—the last solitary fly that buzzed about the pane. "You see, I must live on a little longer."

She did live; ay, until, as I once heard her say—and the words have followed, and will follow me all my life, like a benediction—she had been made to "enjoy" living.

But that was long, long afterwards. Now, for many months, nay years, the desolate woman fell into that stupefied state which is scarcely living at all. I will not, I dare not describe it, but many people have known it—the condition when everything about us seems a painted show, among which we move like automaton figures, fulfilling scrupulously our daily duties, eating, drinking, and sleeping; answering when we are addressed, perhaps even smiling back when we are smiled upon, but no more really alive, as regards the warm, breathing, pleasure-giving, pleasurable world, than the dead forms we have lately buried, and with whom half our own life has gone down into the tomb.

It was so—it could not but be—with the

childless mother, left alone in her empty house,
or worse than alone.

How much Sir Edward felt the death of his
children, or whether he missed them at all, it
was impossible to say. Outwardly, their loss
seemed to affect him very little, except that he
sometimes exulted in having his wife's continual
company, and getting her "all to himself," as
he said.

He was very fond of her, no doubt of that—
fonder than ever, it appeared; and as if in some
sort of compenstion, he became much less troublesome, and far easier to manage. His fits
of obstinacy and violence ceased; in any difficulty she had unlimited influence over him. His
inherent sweet temper returned in the shut-up
life he led; no temptations from outside ever
assailed him, so that all Josephine's old anxieties from her husband's folly or imprudence
were for ever at an end. He never interfered
with her in the smallest degree, allowed her to
manage within and without the house exactly
as she chose; was content just to be always be-

side her, and carry on from day to day an existence as harmless as that of a child, or what
they call in Ireland a "natural."   He was never
really mad, I believe, so as to require restraint
—merely silly; and the constant surveillance of
his wife, together with her perfect independence
of him in business matters, prevented the necessity of even this fact becoming public.   Upon
the secrets of his melancholy illness no outside
eye ever gazed, and no ear heard them afterwards.

The forlorn pair still lived on at Brierley Hall.
Sir Edward could not, and, fortunately, would
not, be removed from thence: nor did Lady de
Bougainville desire it.   If she had any feeling
at all in her frozen heart, it was the craving to
see, morning after morning, when she rose to
begin the dreary day, the sun shining on the
tall spire of Brierley church, under the shadow
of which her three daughters lay : her three sons
likewise, in time ; for after some years she had
them brought home from Switzerland, and laid
there too, to sleep all together under the honey-

scented, bee-haunted lime-trees which we are
so proud of in our Brierley churchyard.

In the early days of her desolation she had
parted with Oldham Court, according to the
conditions—which she and her son César had
once laughed at as ridiculously impossible—of
Mr. Oldham's will. She sold the estate, but
not to a stranger; for another impossibility, as
was thought, also happened. Lady Emma, so
tenderly cherished, lingered several years, and
before she died left a son—a living son—for
whom his father had bought the ancestral property, and who, taking his mother's maiden
name, became in time Mr. Oldham of Oldham
Court. When Lady de Bougainville heard of
this, she smiled, saying, "It is well," but she
never saw the place again, nor expressed the
slightest desire to do so. Indeed, from that
time forward she never was ten miles distant
from, nor slept a single night out of, Brierley
Hall.

She and Sir Edward lived there in total seclusion. No guests ever crossed the threshold

of their beautiful house; their wide gardens
and pleasure-grounds they had all to themselves. In summer time they lived very much
out of doors; it amused Sir Edward; and there
were neither children nor children's friends to
hide his infirmities from, so that his wife let him
wander wherever he chose. He followed her
about like a dog, and if left a minute, wailed
after her like a deserted infant. His entire and
childlike dependence upon her was perhaps a
balm to the empty mother-heart. Bridget sometimes thought so.

It was needed. Otherwise, in the blank
monotony of her days, with nothing to dread,
nothing to hope for, nothing to do, in the
forced self-containedness of her stony grief,
and in the constant companionship of that
half-insane mind, Josephine's own might have
tottered from its balance. She used sometimes
to have the strangest fancies—to hear her
children's voices about the empty house, to see
them moving in her room at night. And
she would sit for hours, motionless as a statue,

with her now constantly idle hands crossed on her lap; living over and over again the old life at Wren's Nest, with the impression that presently she should go back to it again and find the narrow, noisy, poverty-haunted cottage just as before, with nothing and no one changed. At such times, if Bridget, who kept as close to her as Sir Edward's presence rendered possible, and kept every one else sedulously away, suddenly disturbed her dream, Lady de Bougainville would wonder which was the dream and which the reality—whether she were alive and her children gone, or they living and she dead.

To rouse her, there came after a while some salutary suffering. In the slow progress of his disease, Sir Edward's failing mind took a new turn. That extreme terror of death which he had always had, became his rooted and dominant idea. He magnified every little ache and pain, and whenever he was really ill fell into a condition of frantic fear. All religious consolations failed him. That peculiar form of doc-

trine which he professed—or rather, that corruption of it, such as is received by narrow and
weak natures—did not support him in the least.
He grew uncertain of what he was once so com-
placently sure of—his being one of the " elect ;"
and, in any case, the thought of approaching
mortality, of being dragged away from the
comfortable world he knew into one he did not
know, and, despite his own poetical pictures of
glory hereafter, he did not seem too sure of,
filled him with a morbid terror that was the
most painful phase of his illness. He fancied
himself doomed to eternal perdition ; and the
well-arranged " scheme of salvation," which he
used to discuss so glibly, as if it were a mere
mathematical problem, and he knew it all, faded
out from his confused brain, leaving only a fearful image of the Father as such preachers describe Him—an angry God, more terrible than
any likeness of revengeful man, pursuing all
His creatures who will not, or cannot, accept
His mercy, into the lowest deep of judgment
—the hell which He has made.   For this, put

plainly—God forbid I should put it profanely!
—is the awful doctrine which such self-called
Christians hold—also, strange to say, many
most real and earnest Christians, loving and
tender, pitiful and just; who would not for
worlds act like the God they believe in. Which
mystery we can only solve by hoping that, under its external corruption, there is a permanent divineness in human nature which makes
it independent of even the most atrocious
creed.

But Sir Edward's religion was of the head,
not of the heart; a creed, and nothing more.
When, in his day of distress, he leant upon it,
it broke like a reed. His feeble mind went
swinging to and fro in wild uncertainty, and
he clung to his wife with a desperation pitiful
to see.

"Don't leave me! not for a minute," he would
say, during their long weary days and dreadful nights, "and pray for me—keep always
praying, that I may not die, that I may be allowed to live a little longer."

Poor wretch! as if in the Life-giver and Life-taker—omnipotent as benign—he saw only an avenging demon, lower even than the God whom, after his small material notions, he had so eloquently described and so patronizingly served. At this time, if she had not had her six children to think of—her children, so loving and loved, whom God could not have taken in anger; who, when the first shock of their death had passed away, began to live again to her, as it were; to wander about her like ministering angels, whispering, "God is good, God is good still:" but for this, I doubt, Josephine would have turned infidel or atheist.

As it was, the spectacle of that miserable soul, still retaining consciousness enough to be aware of its misery, roused her into a clear, bold, steady searching out of religious truth, so far as finite creatures can ever reach it. And she found it—by what means, it is useless here to relate, nor indeed would it avail any human being, for every human being must search out truth for himself. Out of the untenable negation, to which her

husband's state of mind led, there forced itself
upon hers a vital affirmative : the only alternative
possible to souls such as that which God had
given her—a soul which longs after Him, cannot exist without Him, is eager to know and
serve Him, if He only will show it the way ; but
whether or not, determinedly loving Him : which
love is, to itself, the most conclusive evidence of
His own.

I do not pretend to say that Lady de Bougainville was ever an "orthodox" Christian : indeed,
unlike most Christians, she never took upon herself to decide what was orthodox and what
heterodox ; but a Christian she became ; in faith
and life, and also in due outward ceremonial ;
while in her own spirit she grew wholly at
peace. Out of the clouds and thick darkness in
which He had veiled Himself, she had seen God
—God manifest in Christ, and she was satisfied.

"It is strange," she would say to Bridget,
when coming for a moment's breathing space
out of the atmosphere of religious despair
which surrounded poor Sir Edward—"strange,

but this gloom only seems to make my light grow stronger. I used to talk about it—we all do—but never until my darlings were there, did I really believe in the other world."

And slowly, slowly, in the fluctuations of his lingering illness did she try to make it as clear to her husband as it was to herself. Sometimes she succeeded for a little, and then the shadows darkened down again. But I cannot, would not even if I could, dilate on the history of this terrible time, wherein day by day, week by week, and month by month, Josephine was taught the hardest lesson possible to a woman of her temperament, patiently and without hope to endure.

There is a song which of all others my dear Lady de Bougainville used most to like hearing me sing; it is in Mendelssohn's Oratorio of "St. Paul": "Be thou faithful unto death, and I will give thee a crown of life." I never hear it, with its sweet, clear tenor notes dying away in the words "Be thou faithful—be thou faithful unto death," without thinking of her. She was "faithful."

Sir Edward had a long season of failing health; but at last the death of which he was frightened came upon him unawares. The old heart disease, which had once been so carefully concealed from him, after lying dormant for years, till his wife herself had almost forgotten it, reappeared, and advanced quicker than the disease of the brain. It was well. That final time of complete idiocy, which the doctors warned her must be, and to which, though she kept up her strength to meet it, she sometimes looked forward with indescribable dread, would never come.

Her husband woke up one night, oppressed with strange sensations, and asked, as his daughter Adrienne had asked, but oh! with what a different face,—" Can this be dying?"

It was; his wife knew it, and she had to tell him so.

Let me cover over that awful scene. Bridget was witness to it, until even she was gently thrust away by her beloved mistress, who for more than an hour afterwards until seclusion was no longer possible, locked the door.

Towards morning, the mental horrors as well as the bodily sufferings of the dying man abated a little; but still he kept fixed upon his wife that frightened gaze, as if she, and she only, could save him.

"Josephine!" he cried continually, "come near me—nearer still; hold me fast; take care of me!"

"I will," she said, and lay down beside him on the bed—her poor husband, all she had left in the world!—almost praying that it might be the will of God to lengthen out a little longer his hopeless, useless life, even though this might prove to herself a torture and a burthen greater than she could bear. But all the while she felt her wish was vain: that he must go—was already going.

"Edward," she whispered, and took firm hold of the nerveless hand which more than thirty years ago had placed the wedding-ring upon her finger—"Edward, do not be afraid; I am close beside you—to the very last."

" Yes," he said, " but afterwards ? Where am I going ? Tell me, where am I going ? Or go with me. Can you not go with me ? "

" I wish I could !" she sobbed. " Oh, Edward, I wish I could !"

Then again she told him not to be afraid. " Say 'Our Father,' just as the children used to do at night. He is our Father. He will not harm you, He will only teach you—though how, I do not know : but surely, surely He will ! Edward—husband," pressing closer to his ear as the first struggles of death came on, and the blindness of death began to creep over his eyes. " There is nothing to be afraid of : God is good."

And then, when speech had quite failed him, Josephine crept down on her knees beside the bed, and repeated in her sweet, clear voice, "Our Father, which art in heaven," to the end.

The words, comprehensible to the feeblest intellect, yet all that the sublimest faith can arrive at, might have reached him, or might not, God knows! but the dying man's struggles ceased, and a quiet look, not unlike his daughter Adrienne—the one of his children who most resembled him—came over his face. In that sudden "lightening before death" so often seen, he opened his eyes and fixed them on his wife with the gaze almost of her young lover Edward Scanlan. She stooped and kissed him; and while she was kissing him he slipped away, where she could not "take care" of him any more.

Thither—it is not I who dare follow and judge him. Poor Sir Edward de Bougainville!

THE EPILOGUE

—Which perhaps none will listen to. They may say, " The curtain has fallen; the play is played out. No more! "

But the play was not played out. Who dare say, " My work is done," till the breath fails wherewith to say it? Thus, if after her sad and stormy life, it pleased Heaven to give a sunshiny sunset to my dear Lady de Bougainville, why should I not tell it? even though the telling involves more than people may care to hear of this insignificant life of mine—which only became of value after I fell in love with her. But there was once a little mouse who gnawed the netmeshes of an imprisoned lion; and though the creature never pretended to be anything but a mouse, I think it must have been a very happy-minded mouse ever afterwards.

Where shall I take up my story? From the day when she turned the key of the little hair-trunk, thereby silently locking up—as, child almost as I was, I felt that I myself would have locked up—the treasure-house of the past? I asked her no questions, and she gave me no explanations; but from that hour there arose an unspoken tenderness and a sympathy stronger even than that which not seldom draws together the old and the young, in spite of—nay, rather on account of—the great difference between them. Contrast without contrariety is one of the great laws of harmonious Nature; and two people, however unlike, who have the same ideal, will probably suit one another better than many who seem more akin. It was just as when, on reading some great poet—so great yet so simple—I used to be astonished and yet pleased that I could comprehend him. So, I grew worthier and better in my own sight to find I could in a dim, feeble way understand Lady de Bougainville.

Are no love-vows registered except by lovers?
I think there are. I could tell a certain little
maid who lay awake half the night, thinking of
caliphs and viziers, and old trunks with dead
children's clothes; and of what King David said
about the term of mortal life being threescore
years and ten, "and if by reason of strength
we attain unto fourscore years." Ten years
more, then. Ten years to try and fill up a
blank life; to make a dull life cheerful, perhaps
even happy. Ten years for a motherless child
to give passionate, adoring filial duty to the
mother of six dead children; receiving—well,
perhaps nothing; but it mattered not. The
delight was in the duty, not its reward: in
the vow and its fulfilment rather than in the
way it might be accepted by its object. This,
time would show. Meanwhile, in the dead of
night, with the last flicker of flame lighting up
the wan figure of John the Baptist, and the
white owl—which had brought up her young, I
heard, year after year in the ivied courtyard
below—hooting mournfully under the window,

the vow was made. And, thank God! I have kept it to this day.

When I came down at eight o'clock, it was to an every-day breakfast-table, where sat—no, *not* an every-day old lady, talking to an old woman, as broad as she was long, with a kind, good, ugly face, who stood behind her chair. Mistress and servant were, I believe, nearly the same age, but the former looked much the older. They were talking together with that respectful tenderness on one side, and friendly confidence on the other, which marks at once two people who in this relation have spent together nearly all their lives.

Lady de Bougainville looked up as I entered, and turned upon me, a little suddenly, as if she had momentarily forgotten me, her beautiful smile.

I began this book by a picture of her, as near as I could draw it, as she first appeared to me. Now, when I have since tried to paint her in different shape, will the likeness be recognizable? Will any one trace in the stately lady

of seventy, sitting placidly at her lonely breakfast-table, the passionate Josephine Scanlan of
Wren's Nest? Still less will there be read in
the sweet old face—the cheeks of which were
pink and fresh as a girl's, for she had been out
in her garden, she told me, since seven in the
morning—those years of anguish and trial,
ending in the total desolation of the widowed
wife and childless mother, from whom God had
taken everything—everything! leaving her
alive, and that was all?

Strange—inconceivably strange!—and yet
most true. Sometimes—as she showed me
that day in one of her favourite laurels—when
a healthy tree has been blighted by frost, if it
still retains a fragment of vitality it will shoot
up again, not in its old shape, but in a different
one, and thus live on. So did she.

"Bridget," said Lady de Bougainville, "this
is Miss Weston, who has been so very ill, and is
come to us to be made well again. Bridget
will look after you and take care of you, my
dear. She is wonderful at nursing, and

rather likes having somebody to make a fuss over."

Bridget curtsied, with a fond look at her lady; and then, softening a little, I suppose, at my white face—for I was very weak still—hoped with true Irish politeness that I should soon get better; everybody must feel the better for coming to Brierley Hall. In which sentiment I cordially agreed with her. And perhaps she was sharp enough to see my heart in my eyes, for she gradually became mild towards me, and we grew capital friends, Bridget and I.

And Bridget's mistress?

I have a distinct recollection of every hour of that day, the first whole day that I spent with her, and which was the type of many other days; for they were all alike. Existence went on like clockwork in that great, lonely, peaceful, beautiful house. At seven—winter and summer—the mistress was in her garden, where she had a personal acquaintance with every flower and bush and tree, and with every living thing that inhabited them.

"I think," she said to me one day, "I am fonder of my garden than even of my house, because my garden is alive. And it is always busy—always growing. Even at my time of life I like to see things busy and growing."

She was always busy, certainly. To my surprise, directly after breakfast she sat down to her "work;" and very hard work it was, too. First, the management of her household, into the details of which she entered with the minutest accuracy: liberal, but allowing no waste; trustful, but keeping a careful observation of everything. Next, the "stewardship," as she called it, of her large fortune, which entailed much correspondence; for her public and private charities seemed endless. She was the best woman of business I ever knew. She answered her letters every day, and paid her bills every week: "For," she said, "I wish those that come after me to have, when I die, as little trouble as possible."

This solitary living—solitary dying—which she referred to so continually and so calmly, at first seemed to me very terrible. Yet beautiful too; for it was a life utterly out of herself. Sitting at her little writing-table, in her corner by the fire, she seemed for ever planning how, by purse or influence or kindly thoughtfulness, she could help others. " Why not? I have nothing else to do," she said, when I noticed this; and then, as if shrinking from having said too much, or betrayed too much by the sigh which accompanied the words, she began hastily to tell me the history of a letter she was then writing to a certain Priscilla Nunn, for whom she had just bought an annuity.

" I paid it myself for several years, and then I began to think, suppose I were to die first, what would become of Priscilla? So I have made all safe to-day; I am so glad."

She looked glad, with the pure joy that has nothing personal in it; and then, in that pretty garrulousness which was almost the only sign of age about her, began to tell me more of this Priscilla Nunn, and how she, Lady de Bougain-ville, had once sewed for her.

" For money, Winifred. Since, as I told you last night, I was once very poor."

"But you are not sorry to be rich? Not sorry to be able to do such things as you have just now been doing? Oh, it must be grand—grand! To sit in your quiet corner here, and stretch invisible comforting hands half over the world, just like Providence itself. How I envy you! What it must be to have power, unlimited power, to make people happy!"

" God only can do that," she said, gravely.

"Yes; but He uses you to do it for Him."

I know not how the words came into my mouth, but they did come, and they seemed to please Lady de Bougainville. She laid her hand upon mine, very kindly.

" You speak ' wiser than you are ware of;' and even an old woman is not too old to learn wisdom from the lips of a child."

Then she rose, and saying, her work was done for to-day, took me with her into the library.

That library, what a world of wealth it was! in ancient and modern literature, down to last month's reviews and magazines.

"I took to reading, twenty years ago, to keep myself from thinking," said Lady de Bougainville; " and in my long evenings I have taught myself a little of modern languages. But I was never an educated woman. No doubt," she added, with a smile, "you, a modern young lady, know a great deal more than I."

Perhaps I did, having swallowed an enormous quantity of unassimilated mental food; but I was a starved young pedant still, and I had not lived three days with Lady de Bougainville before she taught me the wholesomest lesson a girl of my age could learn—my own enormous ignorance.

Taught it me quite unconsciously, in daylight walks and fireside talks; when, after her long lack of any companionship, even mine, such as it was, proved not unwelcome to that strong, clear brain, which had come to the rescue of the empty heart and saved it from breaking.

Yet there was a good deal of eccentricity about her too, and about her way of life, which had long fallen into such a mechanical round that she disliked the slightest change therein. To press one hour's duties into the next one, to delay or alter a meal, to rise later or go to bed earlier than usual, was to her an actual pain. But these were only the little spots in my sun. She shone still, the centre of her peaceful world; from her radiated all the light it had, and, in its harmony and regularity, I, poor little wandering star that I was! first learnt, in great things and small, the comfort, the beauty, the actual divineness of heaven's first law—Order.

Yet when I lived longer with her, and, my visit over, found some excuse, often so shallow that she actually smiled, for coming to see her nearly every day, it was impossible not to allow that Brierley was right in calling Lady de Bougainville "peculiar." She had some crotchets, absolute crotchets, which one would have smiled at but for the causes which originated them, too sad for any smile. She never would enter a single house in Brierley—that is a well-to-do house, though she often crossed the thresholds of the poor. Nor would she have any visitors of her own rank; she shut her doors, as I once told her, laughing, upon all "respectable" people. Even my father, except for his formal clerical visits, was not admitted there any more than the old rector had been. She seemed to shrink from all association with the outside world—that is, personal association—though she knew all that was going on therein, and liked to hear of events and people, near and remote, in which I tried to interest her. But though she listened, it was always with a gentle indifference, as if that long frozen-up heart, which was kind to all living things, was capable only of kindness, nothing more; the warm throb of responsive human affection being stilled in it for ever.

I often thought so. And when I, in my impetuous youth, used day after day to spring up the entrance-steps, guarded by their two huge

stone vases, and, with an expectation eager as
any of the "fellows" (as Lady G. in "Sir
Charles Grandison" calls them) that used to
came a-courting to the young gentlewomen in
hoops and farthingales who once inhabited
Brierley Hall,—I went in search of my beautiful old lady, my silly heart often sank down
like lead. For, though she always paused in
whatever she was doing, to give me the gentle
"Is that you, my dear? how kind of you to
come and see me," I felt by her very use of the
word, that her heart towards me was only
"kind"—that was all.

Well! how could it be otherwise? What a
foolish girl I was to expect it to be otherwise!
And yet it sometimes made me a little sad to
think I had only the stubble-end of her life while
she reaped the whole rich harvest of mine.
"Ridiculous!" most people would say; "Con-
temptible!" I think she would have said, who
of all women most understood what that love
is which loves freely, hoping for nothing again.
Yet I fretted a good deal about it, until chance

brought my trouble to a climax, and me to my right senses for evermore.

Somebody hinted to my father that I was going too much to Brierley Hall; that people would say I had designs upon the old lady, who had a large fortune and no heirs. So he, being a proud man, dear heart! and a sorrowful, hard life had made him prouder still, when my next invitation came, forbade my going thither.

I rebelled. For the first time in our lives my father and I had words—and bitter words, too. I was not a child now; I was past seventeen, with a strong will of my own; and it was not only my own pleasure that I grieved to lose. Summer had gone by, that long, bright summer when I had been made so happy at Brierley Hall, and grown familiar with every nook within and without it. Now, the bare trees stretched empty arms up to the leaden winter sky, and within the house—the large, chilly, gloomy house—where the Christmas holly smiled forlornly upon the vacant rooms, sat one lonely old woman, who, rich as she was, sweet and loveable as every day I found her more and more to be, was still only a woman, lonely and old.

"I *will* go to her, whatever you say!" cried I, in a passion of tears, and rushed from my father, hardly knowing what I was doing, or what I meant to do—rushed through the stormy afternoon, to Brierley Hall.

Lady de Bougainville was sitting in the cedar parlour, the smallest and least dreary of all the rooms. For a wonder she was doing nothing, only looking into the fire, which had dropped into hollow blackness, as if long un-stirred.

"How good of you, Winny, to come all through the rain! I am quite idle, you see, though I have plenty of work to do. Perhaps it is the fault of my eyes, and not the dark day, but I cannot manage to thread my needle."

She spoke a little sadly. I knew if she had a dread in this world it was of her sight failing her, of growing "dark," as Bridget called it,

which to one so independent in her ways and
disliking dependence more even than old people usually do, would have been darkness indeed.

" Still, if it comes," added she, sighing again
(I knew what " it " meant), " I hope I shall be
able to bear it."

" It will not come, and if it did, you would
bear it," said I passionately, as I sat down on
the footstool beside her, and took possession of
her dear old hand, playing ostensibly with the
emeralds and diamonds which covered it.   But
it was the hand I loved, soft and warm, strong
and delicate, lovely to look at, lovely to feel ; as
I can see and feel it still, though——.   No, I
will have none of these tears.   We may weep
over the blasted, withered corn, the grain trod-
den under foot, or scattered unreaped to the
winds of heaven ; but when the ripe sheaf is
gathered into the garner, then who grieves ?

Let me remember her as she sat in her easy-
chair and I sat at her feet, trying to amuse her
all I could ; with tales of the village, of the

neighbours, of various Christmas treats in the schoolrooms and the almshouses, and so on. To all of which she listened with her usual smile ; and I kept up mine too as well as I could. But I was not good at deception, I suppose, for she said suddenly—

"Winifred, there is something on your mind ; tell me what it is. I should be sorry if any trouble were to come near my merry little Mouse. (Mouse was a name she had for me from my smallness, my bright eyes—yes, I fancy they were bright, being like my father's —and the brown of my hair.)

The kind words—so unexpected—touched me to the quick. Bursting into tears, I poured out to her my grievous woe and wrong.

" Is that all ? What mountains of molehills we do make at seventeen ! To be in such despair from a lost visit ! My silly little girl !" I drew back in sensitive pain. Evidently, the real cause of my grief, the dread I had of being separated from her, and the fact that the chief happiness of my life consisted in being with her, had never occurred to my dear old lady.

It was hard: even now I recognise that it was hard. And I do not hate poor Winny Weston, that the bitterness and anguish of her heart found vent in exaggerated words.

"Silly am I! I know that, and no wonder you think so. It is no matter to you how seldom I see you, or if I am never allowed to see you again. I am nothing to you, while you are everything to me."

A declaration as impetuous as that of any young man in love—nay, I have taunted one young man with its being more so! No wonder Lady de Bougainville was a little astonished by it—until perceiving how real my emotion was, she, with a curious sort of look—

> "Half smiling, half sorry,
> Gazed down, like the angels in separate glory,"

upon poor, foolish, miserable me.

Then she spoke seriously, even sadly:—
"Winny, I had no idea you cared for me so much; I thought no one would care for me again in this world."

While she spoke a quiver ran across her features, and a dimness—I could hardly believe it tears, for I had never seen her shed one—gathered in her eyes.

"You are very good," she said again,—"very good to an old woman like me; and I am grateful."

Grateful! Lady de Bougainville grateful to me? And telling me so with that sweet dignity which made me more than ever ashamed of myself; for had I not heard her say more than once, that the love which worries its object with jealous exactions, is not love, but the merest selfishness?

I hung my head. I begged her pardon. "But," I said, "this is hard on me—harder than you think. What chance have I of learning to be good, and sensible, and womanly, excepting through you? I thought you would have 'grown' me, as you do your young servants and your cabbages."

I had made her smile, which was what I wanted; also, perhaps, to wipe out with a sillier jest the remembrance of my romantic folly.

"And then, as you told me once, no sooner do they get hearts in them, than some young man of Brierley finds it out and carries them off. It would be just the same with you, Winny!"

"Never!" I cried, indignantly; "I wish for nothing better than to spend my whole life beside you."

"Ah, that is what children often say to their parents, yet they marry for all that."

"I never would, if I were a child of yours."

"A child of mine!" The words seemed to pierce her like sharp steel. "You forget I have no children—that is, all my children are in heaven. No one on earth can ever replace them to me."

I had gone too far; I recognised it now. Recognised, too, with a passionate sympathy that almost took away the personal pain, what tenacity of faithfulness was in this strong heart of hers, which admitted no substitutes! Other interests might cluster round it outside, but its inner, empty niches would remain empty for ever.

"No," I said gently—not even attempting to repossess myself of her dear hand, which had slid from mine somehow—"neither I nor any one could ever dream of replacing to you your children. But you will let me be your little servant? I love you so."

She was touched, I saw. Even through the frost of age, and of those many desolate years, she felt the warmth of this warm young love of mine. Stooping down, she kissed me affectionately; and giving me one of her hands, sat, with the other hand shading her face, for ever so long. We made no mutual protestations—indeed I think we hardly exchanged another word on the subject—but from that hour our relations seemed to rest on a different footing, and we understood tacitly that they were to last for life.

I could have sat for ever at her feet, catching glimpses of her face in the firelight, and won-

dering how it felt to have had everything and
lost everything, and to come to sit at seventy
years of age, by a vacant hearth, with all one's
treasures in heaven; and, as the Bible says,
" where one's treasure is, there will one's heart
be also." Wondering, too, whether it was that
which caused the peace that I saw gradually
growing in her face, as at last removing her
hand, she left it for me to gaze at. It was quite
bright now.

" I have made up my little plans, Winny,"
said she cheerfully, "and you shall hear from
me to-morrow—that is, your father shall. Now
go home to him, for it is growing dark, and he
will be anxious. Happy you to have a father
who is anxious over you! We must not vex
him. Parents first, always."

" Yes," I answered, but it might have been a
little dolefully, and more lingeringly even than
usual I might have taken my departure; for
just at the door Lady de Bougainville called me
back.

" Child"—and the hand she laid on my shoulder was firm as that of youth, and her eyes blazed as they might have done thirty or forty years ago. "Child, be wise! Before you sleep, make friends with your father, and be thankful that he is such a father—a prudent, tender, honourable man. All men are not so. Sometimes it is the will of God to tie together, by relationship or marriage, people who are so unlike that, if not thus tied, they would fly from one another to the world's end. And sometimes" —her voice sank lower—" it is a right so to fly. They have to choose between good and evil, between God and man. Pity them, but let no one dare to judge them—no one can—except the Judge of all."

She stopped, trembling violently. Why, I knew not then; I do now. But very soon she recovered herself—the sooner, I think, because she saw that I understood nothing below the mere words she was saying. All I did was to stand shame-faced before her—she, who was so wise, so good; so infinitely wiser and better than I could ever hope to be. I said so.

"No," she answered, sadly; "neither good nor wise. Only one cannot live seventy years and learn nothing. Therefore, Winifred, listen to me. Never say to any one what you said to me to-day—that you wished you could leave your father. Some have to do it, as I said : children from parents, wives from husbands, must turn and depart. And if it has to be done" —and she drew herself erect, and her eyes flashed, almost fiercely, till I could understand what a fierce woman she must have been in her youth—"if it must be done, I say, Do it! unflinchingly, without remorse. Cut off the rotten branch, fly from the plague-stricken house. Save your soul, and fly. But, oh! not till the last extremity, not till all hope is gone—if it ever is quite gone : we cannot tell. Child, those whom God has given you, have patience with them; *He* has. Hold fast by them, if it be possible, to the end."

And as she looked at me, I saw all her fierceness ebb away, and a tenderness, deeper than even its usual peaceful look, grow on her dear face.

"Now go, my child. I have said enough, perhaps too much, but I want you to be friends again with your father. I think," she added— (was it with a natural fear of having betrayed anything, which I understood not then, but do now?)—"I think I am sensitive on the subject of fathers; mine was very dear to me. He died—more than fifty years ago; yet I remember him, and all about that time, more clearly than I remember many nearer things. We were very happy together, my father and I."

She spoke calmly and cheerfully, as it seems people do learn to speak of their dead, after fifty years; and, kissing me, sat down again once more in her quiet arm-chair by her solitary fire.

Next day, my father showed me a letter which he had just received from Lady de Bougainville, asking his permission for me to be

Q 2

her reader and amanuensis for two hours every forenoon. She needed such help, she said, because of her failing eye-sight, and preferred mine, because she was used to me, and "loved" me.

"Not that I wish to monopolize your daughter." (I smiled to see how boldly her noble candour cut the knot that would have perplexed a feebler hand.) "Still less do I intend, as I hear is reported in Brierley, to leave her my fortune. It has been left, for many years, to a charity. But I wish to make her independent, to put in her hand what every woman ought to have—a weapon wherewith, if necessary, to fight the world."

She therefore proposed, instead of salary, to give me first-rate masters of every kind, and that I should take my lessons of afternoons, at Brierley Hall. This would make all easy, she said, during my father's frequent absence from home all day long. "And you may trust me to take care of your child," she added. "I was a mother once."

This last touch went to my father's heart—a tender heart, for all its pride.

" Poor lady—poor lady ! " said he. And after reading the letter over once again, with the comment, " She is a wise old woman, this grand friend of yours," consented to it without reserve.

Thus my life was made plain to me—plain and clear, busy and bright; nay, brighter than I ever expected. For my father himself, on his own account, began to admire Lady de Bougainville.

Hitherto they had held aloof, for they differed widely theologically. She listened to his sermons—never commenting, never criticising—and that was all. But, as she slowly found out, whether or not he preached it, he lived " the Gospel." " Winny," said she to me one day, when she had watched him into one of those miserable cottages which were the disgrace of our parish, where, like most increasing parishes, the new-built palatial residences of our rich neighbours drove our poor neighbours to herd

together like pigs in a sty—"Winny, some of
these days I should like to see a little more of
your father.   Once, I believed in the Church in
spite of the minister; now, I believe in the
Church—and the minister."

And when I told him this, again he said,
"Poor lady!"   For my father, like the late
Reverend Sir Edward de Bougainville—of which
he had chanced to hear a good deal, since he
came here, from an Irish dean he knew—was a
Low Church clergyman.

Low Church, High Church, Broad Church—
what insane distinctions!   Oh, that I could ob-
literate them all!   Oh, that I could make every
one who serves at the altar like this dear father
of mine—whom I do not paint here, for he is
mine, and he lives still, thank God!   He and I
do not agree entirely ; like many another child,
I fancy Heaven has granted to me clearer light
and purer air than to my father; but I love
him!   I love him! and I believe God loves us
both.

And we both of us lived and grew together

in love more and more, under the shadow of that beautiful and benign old age of Lady de Bougainville. I cannot picture it—who could ? —but it was most like one of those November days which always remind me of her; when the whole world seems spiritualized into a sunshiny tranquillity, so that we notice neither sodden leaves nor withered flowers, nor silent gardens empty of birds, but delight ourselves in the celestial beauty of the departing year, as if it were to remain with us for ever.

On just such a day, the 18th of November (for though I did not note the date, others did), something happened which was the first break in the heavenly monotony of our lives, and which therefore, I suppose, I ought to set down, though to me then, and long afterwards, it seemed a matter of little moment.

We had been sitting, Lady de Bougainville and I, in the summer-house by the lake, where we still spent every fine afternoon. She had two " crotchets," she called them, being quite aware of every weakness she had, and now and

then half apologizing for some of them; she
liked to live like a bird in the open air, and
every day to see the last of the sun. He was
setting now, gorgeously, as he often does in
November, in front of us, and making a second
sun-set glow in the yellowing elm-leaves which
still hung on the boughs of the wood behind.
For the park round Brierley Hall was full of
magnificent trees—the relics of the old chase—
and its mistress barricaded herself with them
against those horrible villas which were rising
up, like red and yellow fungi, on every side.
It was her weak point, that and the new rail-
way, now crawling like a snake every day
nearer and nearer, till as we sat here we could
hear the navvies hammering in the cutting below.

It vexed her—even in her calm old age, it
vexed her. She saw no beauty in these modern
improvements, which were making our pretty
village like a London suburb; and she hated,
with an almost amusing wrath—which I rather
delighted in, since it brought her down to the

level of common mortals—every new-built house that lifted up its ugly head, chimney-laden, to stare into her green domain.

"There is another, I declare!" she cried, catching a sight which I had noticed days before, but kept to myself. Now the thinned trees discovered it all too plain. "Look, Winifred, your eyes are better than mine. Are they not building a great, yellow-brick house, with a turret to it, which will overlook us where we sit? Horrible! I never infringe on my neighbours' rights, but I must preserve my own. This must be seen to immediately."

I encouraged her wrath, I fear, for it did my heart good to see it—to find her so much "of the earth earthy." Since these three days, she had been kept indoors with one of the slight illnesses which sometimes came even to her healthy old age, and which she called, with the quaint phraseology she often used, "her messages from home."

So I followed her, smiling to myself, as with a firm, indignant step she walked home, fast as any young woman, and sent a message to the owner, builder, foreman, or whoever was in charge of the obnoxious house, that Lady de Bougainville wished to speak to him immediately.

I smiled then. I smile now, with a strange, half-sad content, to think how little we know what is before us, and upon what merest trifles hang all the momentous things of our lives.

Immediately, as she had requested—indeed so soon that we had hardly time to recover our equilibrium, since even such a small thing as this was an event in our quiet days—appeared a gentleman—yes; Bridget, who saw him waiting in the hall, was certain he was a gentleman —who sent up his card, saying he was the architect of the house opposite.

"Mr. Edward Donelly! An Irish name," said Lady de Bougainville, shrinking back with vainly suppressed repugnance. "I think I would rather not see him. I have not seen a stranger for so many years. Winifred, will you speak to him?"

I might have reasoned, but had long ceased
to reason against those dear, pathetic " peculiarities" of hers—may others have patience with
mine when I am seventy years old! So, un-
hesitatingly—thinking only to save her from
any annoyance, and furious against house, owner, architect, any one who should presume to
annoy her—her, before whom I would have laid
myself down as a mat for her feet to walk over
—I marched into the cedar parlour.

There stood a—yes, he was a gentleman,
though not an elderly one, as I had expected.
He seemed about five or six and twenty, tall—
six feet and more—which gave him a most unpleasant advantage over me, poor furious pigmy
that I was! A worse advantage was his look
of exceeding good-humour, his apparent uncon-
siousness of having offended me or anybody
else in the world. Such a bright, honest, cheerful face, such a pleasant manner! It was irri-
tating to the last degree.

" Lady de Bougainville, I presume? No—I
beg your pardon," and he actually smiled, the

wretch! "She is, I hear, an elderly lady. What does she want with me? Is there any-thing—something about this new house, her messenger thought—in which I can oblige her?"

"Only by pulling it down—every brick of it," cried I, throwing down the gauntlet and rush-ing into battle at once. "You ought to do this, for it overlooks her property and annoys her ex-cessively. And nobody ought to annoy her, at her age, and so good as she is. Nobody ever should, if I could help it."

"Are you her daughter, or niece?" said Mr. Donelly, looking at me in a curious way; no doubt my anger amused him, but he was too polite to show this. And then—without wait-ing for the answer to his question, which per-haps he felt he had no right to put—he went on to explain to me, very quietly and courteous-ly, that his employer, having bought the ground, had a perfect right to build upon it any house he chose, provided it was not obnoxious to his neighbours.

"Which is indeed the last thing he would desire; for, though only a plebeian, as you call him—in fact, a retired tradesman—he is a very worthy fellow. I feel with him, for I also am a self-made man; my father was a mechanic," Mr. Donelly said this with a composure that quite startled me. "But I can feel, too, for Lady de Bougainville, who, I suppose, belongs to the aristocratic class, and is well on in years besides. It must be very trying to her prejudices—I beg your pardon, her opinions—to have to put up with many things of our modern time, which are nevertheless quite inevitable, as they form part of the necessary progress of the world."

"Thank you," said I, "but I did not wish a sermon."—Certainly not from a mechanic's son, I was just on the point of adding, with that bitter little tongue of mine; but when I looked at the young man, something in his frank honesty, combined with a way he had of putting unpleasant truths in the least unpleasant manner, and of never saying a rough word where a smooth one would do, disarmed me. Ay, even though he was an Irishman, had an Irish accent, and an Irish way with him not exactly "blarney," but that faculty which both French and Irish have of turning towards you the sunshiny side of the plum—oiling the wheels of life so as to make them run easily and without grating. And when the plum is thoroughly ripe, and the machinery sound and good, what harm? As Lady de Bougainville once said to me, "You English are very, very good; could you not be a little more what we French call *agréable?* "

He was decidedly agreeable, both in the French and English sense, this Mr. Donelly; and before we parted he made me a promise— very earnestly, too—that he would use his best endeavours with his principal to avoid all annoyance to Lady de Bougainville.

When I told her this, she shook her head. " Was he an Irishman, my dear?"

" I think so."

" Then trust him not," and she grew a shade paler, and set her lips together in their hardest line. "I say nothing against Irishwomen—look at my Bridget, for instance,—but I believe it to be almost impossible for an Irishman either to speak the truth or keep a promise."

Is that quite just? thought I, and should have said so—for I never was afraid of speaking my mind to her now; she liked me all the better for it—but by this time I had heard a good deal, and guessed more, of her history, and knew from what a bitter soil this rank growth had sprung, so I held my tongue. Was it for me to begin to lesson Lady de Bougainville?

Only, with my strong resistance to injustice, even though it were hers, I took some precaution against the fulfilment of her prophecy, and also against her being troubled in any way by the intrusive house. I got my father to go and speak to the owner himself, who would be of course his parishioner, about it. And this resulted in more than I intended, for in the great dearth of educated and companionable men in Brierley, my father and the architect, who was lodging in the village, struck up an acquaintance; and one day Mr. Donelly was actually invited to tea, entirely without my knowledge—indeed I was much annoyed at it at the time, and complained bitterly to Lady de Bougainville at having to entertain a mere mechanic's son.

"You terrible little Tory," said she; "but you will grow wiser in time. Is he an honest man's son? For that is the real question always; and yet not always; good fruit sometimes springs from a worthless tree. Still it is a great mystery, my dear, a great mystery," continued she, falling into that tone of gentle moralizing, which was not unnatural at her age, when life's doing is all done, and its placid thinking alone remains. But she seemed to dislike both thinking and speaking of this Mr. Donelly; I well knew why, and so I ceased to refer to him any more.

Of which, by and by, I was only too glad. Let me, without either sentiment or egotism, get over as fast as I can the next event in my quiet life—a life which, looked back on now, seems so perfect, that a whole year was but as one long sunshiny day.

Mr. Donelly came to our house very often, and—just as I used to come to Brierley Hall—on every excuse he could. My father liked him. So, in degree, did I. That is, I thought him very honest, kind, and intelligent, and was grateful to him for taking such pains to gratify and amuse my father. That was all. As to his thinking of me, in any way but the merest civility, I never suspected it for a moment. Otherwise, I should have kept out of his way, and thereby saved myself many a conscience-smite—the innocent pangs that any girl must feel when she has unwittingly made a man miserable. One day, meeting me in the soft August twilight, as I was walking home from the Hall, having stayed later than my wont—for she was not well, my dear old lady; I was very sad about her—he joined me, and told me he was summoned away that night, probably to go abroad, on some work he had long been seeking, and would I "remember" him until he

came back?   I was so little aware of his meaning that I only laughed and said, " Yes, that I
will, and recommend you too, as the very best
architect I know."   And this unhappy speech
brought about what, he said, he had not otherwise meant to tell me until he had a home to
offer "worthy of me"—that he wished me to
share it.

I suppose men mostly say the same things :
thank God, I never had but one man's wooing,
and that was sad enough to hear ; because of
course, as I did not love him, I could only tell
him so, and refuse him point-blank ; which now
I fear was done ungently and with some disdain-
ful words, for I was taken by surprise.   Marriage was not much in my plan of life at all ;
my own home experience did not incline me in
its favour ; while at the Hall, Bridget inveighed
perpetually against the whole race of men ; and
her mistress kept on the subject a total silence.
If I ever did think of being married, it was to
some imaginary personage like the *preux cheva-*
liers of old.   Though, I was forced to confess,

no mediæval knight could have behaved himself more knightly, with more true courtesy, consideration, and respect, than did this builder of houses, this overseer of bricklayers and carpenters, who perhaps had been one of them himself not so many years ago. Ay, even when I said my last decisive word, looking firmly in his face, for I wished him to make no possible mistake. He was excessively pale, but he pleaded no more, and took his pain with such manly courage that I felt almost sorry for him, and in some roundabout way begged his pardon.

"You need not," he answered, holding our wicket gate open for me to pass in. "A woman's love is quite free, but so is a man's. You are not to blame for having refused me, any more than I am for having asked you. I shall never ask you again, but I shall love you to the day of my death."

So we parted: and I saw no more of him. I never told anybody what had happened; it was only my own affair, and it was better forgotten. Nor, after the first week or so, did I think much

about it, except that when I was tired or sorrowful, or the troubles of life came upon me, as they
did just then, thick and fast—though, as they
only concerned my father and me, and not this
history, I need not specify them—Mr. Donelly's
voice used to come back to me, almost like a
voice in a dream, saying his farewell words, " I
shall love you to the day of my death." And
sometimes, looking in her calm aged face, far,
far beyond all youth's passions and turmoils and
cares, I wondered whether anybody—that Irish
husband, for instance, who, Bridget hinted, had
made her so miserable,—had ever said the same
words, with the same determination and sincerity of tone, to Lady de Bougainville.

Those years, which changed me from a girl
into a woman, made in her the change natural
at her time of life. She had none of Mrs. Thrale's
" three warnings;" her " messages from home"
came still, but softly, tenderly, as such messages
should come to one whose life was so valuable to
everybody about her, so inexpressibly precious, as
she saw, to me. Also, my love seemed to develop

in her another quality, which Bridget said had
not been shown since she was a girl—wife and
mother, but girl still—in Merrion Square ; that
charming *gaieté de cœur*, essentially French, which
made her conversation and her company like
that of a woman of thirty rather than seventy.
And when I was with her I often forgot entirely
how old she was, and reckoned on her future
and my own as if they had been one and the
same.

For we were now permanently settled, my
father being no longer curate, but rector of Brierley. One of Lady de Bougainville's old acquaintances, belonging to the Turberville family, an
Honourable somebody, who wrote her sometimes
the most cordial and even affectionate letters,
happened to be in the Ministry, and the living
was a Crown living; so we always suspected her
of having some hand in its disposal. But she
never owned this, nor any other kind act that it
was possible to do in secret.

This change made mine, as well as my father's, the busiest life possible. Nay, in our

large and growing parish, with my youth and his delicate health, we might both have broken down under our work, save for our neighbour at the Hall. Oh, the blessing of riches, guided by a heart as warm as youth, and a judgment wide and clear with the wisdom and experience of age!

"And are you not happy in all this?" I once said to her. "Is it not well to have lived on to such a blessed, and blessing old age?"

She answered, "Yes."

She was a little less active now than she used to be; had to give up one by one, sometimes with a slight touch of restlesness and regret, some of her own peculiar pleasures—such as her walk before breakfast, and the habit of doing everything for herself, not asking, nay, often disliking, either help or the appearance of help, from those about her. But she let me help her now a little. And, sometimes, when I fetched her her bonnet or fastened her shawl, she would say to me smiling, "My dear, I think I am something like the Apostle Peter: when I

was young, I girded myself and walked whither I
would; now I am old, another girds me and
leads me whither I would not. No, nobody could
do that ;" and, half laughing, she drew herself
up erect. " I am afraid I shall have a pretty
strong will to the last."

Now and then people said to me—those who
saw her at church, and the poor folk who came
about the Hall—that " my Lady" was looking
much older. But I could not, and would not
see it. Whatever change came, was so gradual,
so beautiful, like the fading of that Virginian
creeper which we admired every autumn upon
the walls of her house, that it seemed only
change, not decay. And every feebleness of
hers was as dear to me as the helplessness of a
child is to its young mother, who the more she
has to do for it, loves it the better.

Oh, why is it not always thus ? Why cannot
we all so live ?—I think we could if we tried—
that we may be as much missed at eighty as at
eighteen ?

Though her bodily activity was circumscribed,

Lady de Bougainville's mental energy was as
keen as ever. She and my father laid their
heads together over all the remediable evils in
the parish, and some which had hitherto been
thought irremediable : one I must name, for it
brought about another event, which I had good
cause to remember.

One day my father came to the Hall in perfect
despair upon an old grievance of his, the want
of house accommodation for his poor.

"What chance have I ?" said he, half in anger,
half in grief. "How can I take care of my
people's souls when nobody looks after their
bodies ? What use is it to preach to them in
the pulpit and leave tracts at their doors, and
expect them to be clean and tidy, honest and
virtuous, when they are packed together like
herrings in a barrel, in dwellings ill-drained, ill-
ventilated, with the damp running in streams
down the walls, and the rain dropping through
holes in the roof? For the old houses go un-
repaired, and the new-built ones, few as they
are, are almost worse than the old. I declare

to you I would not put an old horse or even a
dog of mine into some I have seen to-day."

" Will nobody build ?" asked quietly Lady de
Bougainville.

" I have put that question to every land-owner
in the place, and they all say ' No ; it would increase the poor-rates. Besides, cottage property is sunk capital ; it never pays.' Yet they go
on living in their ' elegant mansions ' and their
' commodious villa residences.' Oh you rich ! you
rich ! how you do grind the faces of the poor."

" Hush, father," I whispered, for in his excitement he had quite forgotten himself. But Lady
de Bougainville only smiled.

" You are right, Mr. Weston : that is, right in
the main, though there may be something to
be said on the opposite side—there usually is.
But I thank you for speaking so plainly ; tell
me a little more."

" There is nothing to be told. It is a hopeless matter. Oh, that I had an acre of ground,
or a thousand pounds in my pocket, that I might
build, if only three cottages, where decent work-

ing men might live and work! For charity begins in small things, and, to my thinking, it
generally begins at home."

Again she said "You are right," and sat for
some minutes thinking; then called me. "Winny, how much was that money you put into the
bank for me yesterday? I forget: I am afraid I
often do forget things now."

I told her the sum, a good large one, which
had given her much pleasure at the time, for it
was a debt unexpectedly repaid. I had entreated her to spend it on building a new con-
servatory, for the old one was too far from the
house in wintry weather, and she was so fond
of her flowers. But she had pertinaciously refused. "What, build at my age, and for my
own pleasure? Let us think of something else
to do. Opportunity will soon come." And it
did.

"Mr. Weston, I thank you for putting this
into my mind—for showing me what I ought
to do. I wonder I never thought of it before.
But," and she sighed, "I have been thinking

too much and doing too little, this many a year. Well, one lives and learns—lives and learns. If you like, you shall have that two-acre field behind my stable-yard, and Winny will pay you that money; she knows all about it;—so that you may build your cottages at once."

I knew better than my father how costly the gift was, to her who was so tenacious of her privacy, who liked to hide behind her park and trees, keeping the whole world at bay: but having once decided, the thing was over and done. She entered into the scheme with all the energy of her nature; and wished to set about it immediately, "For," she said, "at my age I have no time to lose."

Lengthy was the discussion between her and my delighted father how best to carry out their plans, doing most good and avoiding most evil.

"For the greatest evil in this sort of scheme," she said, "is making it a matter of charity. Remember, Mr. Weston, my tenants must pay me their rent. I shall exact it punctually, or I

shall turn them out.   I am, or I have sometimes
been called, a hard woman : that is, I help only
those who help themselves, or those whom Providence forbids to help themselves.   The inter-
mediate class, who can help themselves and
will not, the idle spendthrift, the willing bor-
rower, the debtor who is as bad as a thief,
against these I set my face as a flint.   For
them expect of me no mercy ; I have none."

As she spoke the fierce flash, so seldom seen
now, came again into her eyes.   She was much
agitated; more so than the matter in question
required, and my father regarded her in some
surprise.   Then he seemed all at once to remember, and said gently, " No, you will not be
tried.   There is justice in what you say.   ' He
that will not work, neither shall he eat,' for he
would only take the bread out of the mouths of
those that do work.   It is God alone who is so
perfect that He can send His sun to shine upon
both the evil and the good."

Lady de Bougainville was silent, but a slight
blush, so pretty in an old lady, grew upon her

cheek, and she looked at my father with that
tenderness with which she often regarded him,
even when doctrinally she differed from him
most.

They went on planning, and I reading;
though my mind often wandered away, as
young folks' will. I do not know if the mention of building houses carried it away in any
particular direction, but I was considerably
startled when I heard from my father's lips a
certain name which had been unuttered among
us for more than two years.

"Winny, have you any idea what has become
of that young man—Donnell, wasn't his name?
no, Donelly—who built Mr. Jones's house?"

"No," I said, feeling hot all over, and thankful it was twilight.

"Because, Lady de Bougainville, he would
be the very man to design your cottages. He
was full of the subject. Sprung from the people, he knew all about them. And he was so
clever, so honest, so conscientious. Winny, do
try to think how we could get to him."

" He went abroad," I said.

" But he may be back by this time, and Jones might know his address. In any case I should like to hear of him again—such a fine young fellow. And a rising, not a risen man—which you know you would like best, Lady de Bougainville."

Here was a predicament! To explain the whole truth, and hinder a young man's obtaining employment because he had once dared to make love to me; the thing was ridiculous! And yet to have him coming here, to meet him again, as I must, for I was Lady de Bougainville's right hand in everything; what should I do? While I sat considering, whether for half a minute or half an hour, I knew not, being so painfully confused, the decision was taken out of my hands. Lady de Bougainville, in her quick mode of settling things—she never "let grass grow under her feet"—rang the bell.

" Take my card across to Mr. Jones and say I should be much obliged if he would write on it the address of his architect, Mr. Donelly."

Well! it was she who did it, she and Fate; I
had no hand in the matter, and whether I was
glad or sorry for it I did not quite know.

Nor did I, when two days after Lady de Bougainville told me she had had a letter from
him.

"A capital, sensible, practical letter; you can
read it, my dear. And he loses no time too,
which I like. He says he will be down here in
an hour from now. I suppose I must see him
myself—and yet——"

She was visibly nervous—had been so all the
morning, Bridget said; and no wonder. "My
lady has not had a stranger in the house for
twenty—no, it's five-and-twenty years."

A stranger and an Irishman; which latter
fact seemed to recur to Lady de Bougainville,
and haunt her uncomfortably till the minute Mr.
Donelly was announced. Then repeating to
herself, "This is unjust—unjust," she rose from
her chair, and taking my arm ("You will come
too," she had said; "I dislike strangers,") she
crossed with feebler steps than usual the hall,

and ascended the beautiful staircase to the tapestry-chamber. There, looking greyer and
more shadowy than ever in the dimness of the
rainy morning, the painted knights and ladies
reined in their faded steeds, and the spectral
Columbus pointed out for ever, to an equally
ghostly Queen Isabella, his discovery of the
New World.

Standing beneath it—investigating it apparently with the keenness of a young man to
whom the whole world was new, with everything in it to win—stood Edward Donelly.

He was a good deal altered—older, graver,
browner; but it was the same face—pleasant,
honest, kind. I did not like to look at it much,
but merely bowed—as he did likewise, without
offering to shake hands with me—and then I
crept away into the farthest window-seat I could
find.

Thence I watched him and Lady de Bougainville as they stood talking together, for they
fell into conversation almost immediately. At
first it was about the tapestry. which he exces-

sively admired, and she took him round to examine piece by piece, before she entered into
business talk at all. Then they sat down opposite to one another, and launched into the
great cottage question at once.

She liked him, I could see, even though the
Irish accent seemed now and then to make her
wince, and bring a grave, sad, absent look to
her dear face; until some word of his, wise
and generous, honest and manly—and the
subject in hand called out a good many of the
like—made her turn back to him, inquisitively,
but not unkindly, and listen once more. He
had a good deal to say, and he said it well:
earnestly too, as if his whole heart were in it.
His energy and enthusiasm seemed not to dis-
please her, but rather to arouse in her a certain
sympathy, reminding her of something which
had once been in herself, but was no longer.

They talked, I think, for nearly two hours;
by that time the matter was quite settled; and
he departed.

"Yes, I like him," she said, when he was

gone; and he lingered not a minute after their business talk was ended. "Your father was right; I will trust Mr. Donelly, though he is an Irishman."

So he came, all that spring, whenever sent for, and oftener when necessary, to Brierley Hall. Never to Brierley Rectory. My father's cordially given invitations were as cordially but invariably declined. When he and I chanced to meet, his manner was distant, courteous, yet so self-possessed that I began to doubt whether he had not forgotten all about that painful little episode, and whether it was necessary for me to keep so carefully out of his way. He seemed to be absorbingly full of his work—perhaps also he was married. Should I have been glad to hear he was married? I dare not tell. Nay, had she, who was my visible conscience, and before whom I often now felt a sad hypocrite—had Lady de Bougainville herself asked me the question I could not have told.

But she asked me no questions at all; apparently never thought about me, being so engrossed in her cottages. They grew day by day under our eyes, as fast as a child or any other living thing, and she took as much pleasure in them. For they were, as she sometimes said, not dull dead bricks and mortar, but tangible blessings, and would be so to many after she was gone. To make them such, she entered, in concert with Mr. Donelly, into the driest details—saw that windows would open and doors shut—that walls were solid and roofs substantial—that the poor man should have, according to his needs, as many comforts as the rich.

"I don't expect to gain much by my investment," she said to her architect one day, "but I hope not to lose. For I mean, as you say, to do nothing for mere charity. The honest, steady, deserving, who pay me their rent regularly, shall be made as happy as I can make them; the drunken, idle, and reckless may go. Mercy to them is injustice to the rest."

"I know that," he answered. "And yet," turning to her as she stood, and looking right in her face with his honest eyes, " if things came to the worst, in you, of all others, I think would be found that charity which ' suffereth long, and is kind.' "

They often talked on this wise, and upon other than mere business topics; and I stood listening; quite apart, perhaps even a little jealous, yet not altogether miserable. One likes to feel that a man who has once cared for one, is not, at any rate, a man to be ashamed of.

It was on this day, if I remember right—when they had talked until he had missed his train— that Lady de Bougainville first invited Mr. Donelly to lunch. What made her do it I cannot guess, for it was twenty years and more since any guest, save myself, had taken a meal at her table. He accepted, though with hesitation; and we found ourselves sitting all three in the cedar parlour, and doing our best to talk unconstrainedly. She, most; though I saw by her face—the expression of which I knew so well—that every word was painful to her, and that she would have rescinded the invitation if she could.

Nevertheless, when lunch was announced, she, with a smile of half apology to me, took the arm of her guest, and proceeded to the dining-room.

I like to remember these little things, and how I followed these two as they walked slowly across the hall between the green scagliola pillars. A goodly pair they were—for she was, proportionately, almost as tall as he, and as upright. They might have been mother and son, or grandmother and grandson; had her elder children lived she would probably have had a grandson just his age. I wondered, did she think of this? Or, when she took the head of her long table—with him and me on either side, for the seat at the foot was never filled—did she recall the days when the empty board was full, the great silent room noisy with laughter? But whatever she felt, she shewed nothing. I can see her this minute, sitting grave and sweet in her place—which it had pleased Heaven she should occupy so long—leaning over from one to the other of us two, so lately strangers, and talking—as she might have leaned and talked to us out of the other world, to which it often seemed as if she already half belonged.

Mr. Donelly had the most of her talk, of course; and it ranged over all subjects, except "shop," which for the nonce she delicately ignored. Close as they were to her heart, she never once referred to her cottages. Her conversation with him was simply that of a lady with a gentleman, who, however differing from her in opinion, and he held amazingly fast to his own, was a gentleman, and should be treated as such. And he treated her—well, I doubt if any of the old De Bougainvilles could have shown more chivalric deference, more tender respect, than Mr. Donelly always paid to my dear old lady.

But they fought a good deal, these two candid people; and at last, in their lively battles, they got upon a topic which half frightened me. It was about Mr. Jones, the retired tradesman, from whom, of all the inhabitants of the obnoxious villa-residences, Lady de Bougainville seemed most to shrink.

"Nor do I wonder at it," said Mr. Donelly. "He is a rough, coarse, illiterate man, who tries to hide his deficiencies under great show of wealth. But he is an honest-meaning man for all that, and carefully gives to his children the advantages he misses in himself. The girls are well-educated; the boys will all be sent to college. A generation hence the Jones's may be a notable family : they will certainly be an accomplished and refined one."

"Do you think so?"

"I think it, because I feel it. You will see."

"I shall not see," said Lady de Bougainville gently; "but I am glad to believe it. In my old age I believe many things which I doubted when I was young. And I will believe this," with one of her slight bends of old-fashioned compliment, "just because Mr. Donelly says it."

The pretty civility was lost upon him. Alas! he was too much in earnest.

"Do not mistake me, Lady de Bougainville. Do not suppose I undervalue birth or breeding. To be well-born, and gently nurtured, must be" —here he sighed—"one of the greatest blessings that can happen to a man. But it is only a chance blessing; and he to whose lot it does not fall must learn to do without it. I think he can. Perhaps—or, at least, I used to dream so when I was a boy—perhaps the next best thing to being the descendant of an ancient and honourable family is to be the founder of one."

"A better thing, it seems to me," said Lady de Bougainville.

We had risen from table, and were standing in the door-way. He, as he spoke, had drawn himself up to every inch of his excellent height, throwing his shoulders back, a trick he had, and looking out half sadly, yet quite fearlessly, as if right into the unknown future, with those clear good eyes of his. She paused a minute, met them, and then for the first time (they had hitherto only bowed, French fashion) she extended to him her hand. It was taken—reverently, gratefully, almost tenderly; and they again passed on before me arm-in-arm down the long hall.

As they went I overheard—I hardly know how, for it was evidently not meant for me to hear, only I was so painfully alive to all their words—the following conversation:

She said to him, apologizing slightly for the curiosity which an old lady may show, not ungracefully, in a young man's affairs, " You speak of founding a family : are you married ?"

" No."

" But, perhaps, you expect to be ?"

" I do not." He hesitated a little, then added, " Since the matter concerns no one but myself, I will be candid with you. I once asked a lady, and she refused me. I shall never ask again. My profession must be to me in the stead of a wife."

" That is a pity. The lady has had a

loss ; you would have made a good husband."

" Thank you."

They said no more, and she respected his confidence ; for in discussing him afterwards with me, freely as was her habit, this was the only part of Mr. Donelly's conversation which she omitted to speak of. But she spoke very kindly of him ; and next time he came her manner was sweet and gracious as it had never been before : " Because," she said, " young as he is, I respect him. He has taught me another of my lessons. Child, as I once told you, I think we have never done learning."

Was I learning too? I know not. I seemed to live week after week in a curious sort of dream—sometimes happy, sometimes unhappy —in which I was always expecting or dreading something, and not knowing one day what might happen the next.

At last something did happen, though I was ignorant of it at the time.

Mr. Donelly was again invited to lunch and spend the day—indeed I had to write the note of invitation, Lady de Bougainville just signing it, as was her way with much of her correspondence now. For the first time he failed in an appointment, but next day sent her a letter, a rather long letter, which, instead of showing to me, she put in her pocket, saying she would tell me about it another time. That time never arrived, though I remained with her till evening.

All day she was *distrait* and anxious-looking, falling into her old moods of absence and silence. Nay, the slight "peculiarities"—little restless-nesses, obstinacies, and irritabilities, which she had had when first I knew her, and which had since been smothered down into the exceeding serenity of her lovely old age, revived again. That new, vivid interest of her life—her pet cottages, seemed almost forgotten, and she kept dwelling continually upon things long gone by.

It was that day she told me, for the first time, the story of her seven years' secret, and how much the keeping of it had cost her.

"Not that I regret anything, my dear, or doubt that I was right in keeping it. But even a righteous secret is a heavy burthen, and I am sorry for all who have to bear it."

She looked at me and looked away, then referred to herself again, and began speaking of her early poverty, and of other portions of her life at Ditchley, after a fashion that she had never done before, half-accounting for this by saying that I was not a child now, and that she liked to talk of the past to me, if I did not mind.

"I had no youth myself, you know, I married so early. Early marriages are not always safe things; nay, as Bridget would tell you—a thorough misogamist is poor Bridget!—all marriages are a great risk. My wonder is, not that they are sometimes unhappy, but that they are ever happy at all. I should counsel no young girl to change her state unless she thoroughly knows, and deeply loves, the man she marries; and"—patting my cheek—"I should be so sorry to see any trouble come to my little Winifred, that I am glad she cares for no man, and will not marry just yet, perhaps never at all."

"Never at all!" I cried, with the utmost sincerity, believing I could love no man alive as I loved her who bent over me, her dear face grown peaceful again, and tender, with the tenderness that only strong natures know.

She smiled, and went on talking in a desultory way; chiefly about herself, betraying rather than confessing how bright her girlish dreams had been, and how they had melted away like morning clouds; and she had to take up the fragments of her broken life, and carry on through rain and storm, heat and frost, till she came, a lonely old woman, to the evening grey.

"No, not grey," I said, "but a rosy sunset, like that one"—and I pointed westward, whence, through all the six windows of the tapestry-chamber, streamed a flood of yellow light, in which the dim figures looked almost alive. "You are like Columbus, sailing towards the sunset, and seeing it before you—oh, so bright!"

"Yes, and when he had sailed far, far west— do you remember?—and he and his crew were almost exhausted, they perceived, a long way off, across the sea, the scent of the yet invisible spice grounds. And they took courage, for they knew they were not far from land."

She spoke half to herself, with that wistful look, not of this world at all, in her eyes. Frightened, I clung to her, and begged her "not to talk like that, for I almost saw her wings growing." And for days after then, in the anxiety of watching her—for something had vexed her, Bridget said, and brought on one of her brief attacks of illness—I forgot all about Mr. Donelly and the letter.

Nor for some weeks did anything revive the subject. He came but little to the Hall, and never when I was there; though, as I discovered accidentally, he and Lady de Bougainville met frequently at the now nearly finished cottages, and were the best friends in the world. "I never thought my Lady would have taken so to any young man," commented Bridget, "and he an Irishman too. Well, wonders will never cease." But as my dear old lady never said a word to me about him, of course I held my tongue.

Gradually, a queer sort of jealousy came over me. Jealousy of whom, or why? I could not clearly tell—only it made me thoroughly miserable. Something, or some one, seemed to have come between me and her, whom I had been used to engross entirely, and I could not bear it. I never complained, being too proud for that; but all the brightness seemed taken out of my life. I moped about; even my father noticed how ill I was looking; and then I tried an unnatural cheerfulness. For I felt not only ill but wicked, hating everybody about me, and most of all myself. And I suffered—oh, how we do suffer when we are young!

Did Lady de Bougainville notice it? or did she, in her calm old age think nothing of it, concluding my troubles would soon pass away:

hers were all over now. At times I fancied so,
and almost envied her, and those whose life is
completed, whose story is told; for whom no
more sorrow is possible any more.

"No," she said one day, when I had crept to
her footstool, and laid her hand on my hot head,
"it is quite true; nothing does grieve me now;
not very much. In old age one sees farther and
clearer than younger people do. It is like living
on a hill-top, from whence the ups and downs
of life appear in their just proportions, and
every way one looks, one beholds, as it were,
'the crooked straight, and the rough places
plain.'"

A good deal more she said, to the same effect,
which made me weep a little, but not so as to
trouble her. And we sat a long time together,
feeling nearer than we had for some time,—when
our talk was broken in by a sudden visitor—
Mr. Donelly.

Evidently Lady de Bougainville had not expected him, for she started, almost as much as
he did at the sight of her and me together;

and both—nay, we all three—looked extremely uncomfortable.

He apologised hurriedly for his intrusion, saying it was inevitable.

"I have got that work abroad I told you of,
and ought to be off to India in four days; if you
will allow me to transfer to a friend the com-
pletion of your cottages. They are nearly done
now. It is a serious matter, this engagement;
it would last ten years. Will you set me free
to accept it?"

"Certainly," she replied. "Come with me
into the cedar parlour, and explain all."

The explanation took very long, or it seemed so. I scarcely stirred from my seat, I remember, but stupidly watched the light fade,
and the merry spring-birds drop into silence,
until Lady de Bougainville came back and told
me he was gone; and I recognised that, in all
human probability, I should never see him again
in this world. Never! since he had left a formal
message of farewell to my father and me.

Lady de Bougainville delivered it, and then sat
down, silent and sorry.

"Yes, I am sorry he is gone," she owned. "I
like him. Latterly, I have taken great pains to
make friends with him, so as to know him well,
and I like him. He has the true, warm Irish
heart, and a conscience besides; the winning
Irish pleasantness, and sincerity underneath it.
I tested him, and he has not disappointed me.
Nay, he has taught me a lesson which, old as I
am, I had need to learn."

What it was I did not ask; it was, indeed,
impossible to speak, for I began crying. She
drew my head against my shoulder. "Poor
little girl!"—then breathed rather than whispered in my ear, "You need tell me nothing. He
told me all."

"Did he? How dared he!" I cried in hot indignation. For I was not myself, and knew
not how I felt or what I was doing. "He has
told you, and you think——"

"I think my little girl did exactly what was
right, and so does he. How could he expect my

Winifred to drop into a man's mouth all in a minute, like a ripe peach from a wall? He was a very foolish fellow, and I told him so."

I was silent.

"But I also think," she continued gently, "that he is a very good fellow, generous and faithful, honest and true. I have found out all about him, from his birth upwards, and found out nothing ill. If you really knew him, possibly you might love him: I don't say you would, but you might. For he is a man you could trust—which is the beginning and end of all real love."

She sighed, and tried to look into my face, but I hid it carefully.

"What is your objection against him? His being a working man's son?"

"No, that would not matter," said I with an earnestness that surprised myself. But I had grown wiser since I had left my teens behind.

"You are right, Winny: his birth could not matter, and ought not, of itself; for he is thoroughly well-educated and refined. Though, I own, having not quite got over my own class-prejudices, it might matter if he had a tribe of unpleasant relations belonging to him. But he has none. He is quite alone in the world—too much alone for such a warm heart. And he has set it irretrievably upon a certain little girl I know. I will not urge you, Winifred: love must come freely, or it is worthless; and if you do not love him, let him go. He will bear it somehow; busy men seldom break their hearts. Only, if he does not marry you, I think he will never marry anybody."

She ceased. The gentle, slow speech, the soft, cold touch of the little hand, what a contrast to the whirl that was going on in my poor heart and head, making me feel as if the room were turning round and round!

"Do I wound or vex you, my dear, by speaking of this? Forgive me: it was only because you have no mother to speak to; a mother, when she can be trusted, is the best friend always. I remember my own daughter "——she stopped suddenly : a sort of convulsion passed over her face, as if, even now, the remembrance was too bitter to bear. "I had rather not tell you of that. My daughter is long since with God."

Yet no mother could be more tender, more sympathizing than she was with me, another woman's child, with not the slightest claim upon her—of blood, at least ; as, putting aside entirely her own past, she tried to help me to unravel my passionate, troubled present. For even then, I hardly knew my own heart—was cruelly uncertain as to what I had best do, or what I wished to do, except to do right. One thing only I was clear about—my intense anxiety never to be parted from her.

"But we must be parted some time," said she, softly ; "and before I go, it would be a comfort to me to give my little girl into safe keeping—to some one who will take care of her, without tyrannizing over her ; who is a gentle and good man, without being a weak man. Child ! if you knew what it is to have the mere sham of a husband—the mockery of a protector, against whom one has to protect oneself, and more than oneself; above all, the misery of bearing and bringing up children, in whom one's utmost terror is to see any likeness to their father! Yet,"—here she broke off in an altogether changed tone;—"Yet, my dear, many women have borne this. I have seen several instances of it in my long life, and I should like to be quite certain before I die that no such lot will befall my little Winifred—as it never will, if she marries Edward Donelly."

And then she said a good deal more for him (I find myself always writing " him " and " her," as if they were the only two people in the world.)   All her words were true, and I knew it.

" Suppose," she whispered, at last, in the playful manner which sat so prettily upon her, " that instead of an old woman making love to you by proxy in this fashion, the young man were to come back and do it himself?"

" He cannot," I said, half amused and yet

dolefully, "it is quite too late. He has gone away for ever."

"Not—not exactly," and her smile broadened into actual mischievousness. "I told him to take a good hour's walk across country, and come here again, after I had sent you away, you obnoxious little person, whom he has been so afraid of offending, that I have seen not half enough of him—to have a quiet cup of tea and a farewell chat with an old lady whom I think he is rather fond of, and who is never likely to see him again in this world. Hark!"—

For we heard a sound on the gravel below— a step which could be only a man's, and a young man's—firm and strong like himself, and yet a little uncertain too. I don't know how or why, but every footfall went into my heart.

"Shall I tell him to go away? or shall I send him in here? Choose. Just one word, my little Winny! Yes, or No?"

I did not say either, but I clung to her sobbing. She kissed and blessed me, not very far from sobbing herself, and went away.

That evening, two young people instead of one, took tea with Lady de Bougainville; but I cannot be expected to remember much that passed at that memorable meal. I am afraid the conversation was very desultory, and not in the least improving. I can only recall the image of her who sat there at the head of her dining-table, for she made it a composite repast —a "hungry" tea—out of compliment to a gentleman who could not be supposed to live entirely upon love. She sat, in her pretty old lady's dress—black silk and pure white cambric, her sweet old lady's face beaming down upon us, with the happy look that people wear who have helped to create happiness, long after their own has slipped away.

My Ned—we agreed between us that I should call him Ned, instead of Edward, which name seemed to grate upon ears that we would not have wounded for the world—my Ned was, as Lady de Bougainville well knew, the most acceptable son-in-law my father could have found : especially as, not to part me from the two dear ones who said they could not possibly do without me, we agreed, for the first year or two, to come and live at the Rectory. Not without a struggle, I think, on Ned's part, and the uncomfortable feeling of a man who comes and hangs up his hat in his wife's father's house; but still my father was such an exceptional person, that it was not really a humiliation or vexation; and Edward Donelly was too honest a man to care for the mere appearance of things. He says, if he ever adopts a crest or a motto, it shall be this: "Never mind the outside."

Of course he did not go to India. Putting aside all other considerations, there happened to be a little girl at hand who would rather have been a poor man's wife all her days, than allowed him to risk health, life, and everything that makes life dear and valuable, in the struggle after fortune that he would have had out there. He declined the appointment, and has never regretted doing so.

Our courtship-days were not long; and we spent a good many of them at Brierley Hall, often close beside its dear mistress. She said she did not mind our love-making: indeed, rather enjoyed it, as all the time she had two people making love to herself! For indeed, Ned did it, in his chivalric way, quite as much as I.

He used to come to Brierley every Saturday and stay till Monday, the only time he could spare from his active busy life. Oh those heavenly Sundays! a peaceful church-going morning, a long afternoon strolling about under the cool green shadow of the trees, or sitting in the summer-house by the lake; whence we used to catch peeps of the house he had built, which he declared was the best bit of architecture he ever planned in his life! Above all, those still twilights in the tapestry-room: for we never left her alone of evenings, but sat with her, and listened to her talk—charming as ever, fresh and youthful and bright. She was more clever and amusing by far than I, and Ned once actually acknowledged this.

Soon—sooner than I liked—but she insisted

upon it, saying she wished to see it with her
own eyes, came our quiet, simple wedding, at
which the only festivities were a dinner to my
poor people, and a tea-party to my school-child-
ren in the grounds of the Hall. My father
married us; and, seeing that it is not defined in
the Prayer-book whether a man or a woman
should give the bride away, Lady de Bougainville undertook that office herself. I see her
now, in her long sweeping dress of grey silk—
worn for the first and only time—her black
velvet cloak, and close white crape bonnet, under which the faded face looked beautiful still.
And I feel the touch of the soft aged hand that
put mine into the young and strong one, which
will hold it safe through life. Afterwards, as
my husband and I walked down the church together, I noticed—and wondered if she did, too
—the sun shining on the white tablet over the
Brierley Hall pew, where, after that long list of
names, came the brief line, "They all rest
here."

All—all! Every one of her own flesh and

blood, upon whom she had built her hope and
joy. Yet she had lived on, and God had given
her rest, too; rest and peace, even in this world.
Ay, and blessedness, poor childless mother, in
blessing other people's children.

It was her earnest wish that she might live to
hold on her knees a child of mine, but we were
a year and a half without one; and that year
and half drew thinner and thinner the slender
thread of life which Time was now winding up
so fast. She was past eighty—how much we
could not tell, nor could she, for she said she
had long lost count of her birthdays; and that
we should have to guess at her age when it required to be noted down—she did not say
where, having quite given up the habit she
once had of constantly referring to her own
decease. And life, even yet, was not only
tolerable, but even pleasant to her: her few
bodily infirmities she bore so sweetly, and her
mind was so exceedingly youthful still. Only
at times, when recurring, with a memory wonderfully vivid, to events and persons of her

youth, now become historical, she would suddenly recognise how long she had lived, and how she stood, a solitary landmark of gone-by years, in the midst of this busy, bustling world.

"I scarcely belong to this age," she would say. "It is almost time we were away, I and Bridget, before we give anybody trouble."

And poor Bridget, who had far more of the weaknesses of age—mental and bodily—than her mistress, was often tended and soothed by her in a half pathetic, half humorous way, and laughed at, not unkindly, as a "dear, grumbling old woman," which made Bridget laugh too, and, recovering all her Irish good-humour, strive to bear more patiently the inevitable burthen of old age, saying, as she watched the beloved figure moving about—graceful even yet, though active no longer—"Sure enough, my lady isn't young herself, and has a deal to put up with without being bothered by me. But she always did take care of everybody except herself."

And when the time came that I was rather helpless too, Lady de Bougainville turned the tables, and insisted upon taking care of me. She arranged my whole paraphernalia of little clothes, cutting out most of them with her own clever hands, which had once fabricated so many. And her latest skill and latest eyesight were expended upon a wonderfully-embroidered christening robe for little "Josephine," as we were determined to call her from the very first, resolutely ignoring the possibility of her being " Joseph." We used to sit and talk of her for hours, until she grew to us an actual existence.

" I never was a god-mother in my life," Lady de Bougainville said one day, when we sat together with our basket of work between us. " I mean to be quite proud of my god-daughter and name-child. But I shall not leave her a fortune, you know that—neither her nor her mother ; I shall only leave you enough to keep the wolf from the door," and she smiled. " The rest your husband must earn ; he can, and he will. It does a man good, too—makes twice a man of him—to feel he is working for wife and child, and that upon him rests the future of both. Mr. Donelly said so to me only yesterday."

"Did he?" cried I, with my heart in my eyes—the heart so hard to win; but Ned had it wholly now. "I don't very much care for his making a great fortune, but I know he will earn a great name some of these days. And he is so good, so good! Oh, it's a grand thing to be every day more and more proud of one's husband!"

I had forgotten to whom I was speaking—forgotten the painted face over the fireplace behind me— the poor, weak, handsome face, with its self-satisfied smirk, which, wherever she sat, she never looked at, though sometimes it haunted me unpleasantly still.

"Yes," she answered, in a grave, calm tone, neither glancing at it—though it was just opposite to her—nor away from it. "Yes; it is a good thing to be proud—as you are justly proud —of your husband."

I was silent: but I recognised—I, a wife, and

nearly a mother—as I had never done before, how terrible must have been the burthen—the heaviest that can be laid upon any woman— which this woman had had to take up and bear all her life. Ay, and had borne, unshrinkingly, to the end.

It was this day, I remember—for I seem now to remember vividly every day of these last weeks—that a strange thing happened, which I am glad now did happen, and in time for me to know of it, because it proved that, though she was, as she said, "a hard woman"—and all the honest tenants of her cottages and the faithful servants of her house blessed her hardness, for they declared it saved them from being victims to the drunken, the idle, and the dissolute—still Lady de Bougainville was not pitiless, even to those she most abhorred.

The afternoon post brought her a letter, the sight of which made her start and turn it over and over again incredulously. I, in passing it on to her, had just noticed that it was a hand unknown to me; a large, remarkable hand, though careless and enfeebled-looking like an old man's writing. As she opened it, an expression came across her face that, in all the years I had known her now, I had never seen before. Anger, defiance, contempt, repugnance, all were there. With hands violently trembling, she put on her spectacles and went to the window to read it alone. Then she came back and touched Bridget on the shoulder.

"He is alive yet: I thought he was dead long ago—did not you? But he is alive yet. Strange! all my own dead, and he only alive! He has written to me."

"Who, my lady?"

"Mr. Summerhayes."

Bridget's half-stupid old age seemed suddenly roused into fury. She snatched the letter from the table, dashed it down and trampled upon it.

"Never heed him, my lady. Don't vex yourself; he isn't worth it. How dare he trouble you? What does he want?"

"What he always wanted—money," and a slight

sneer moved her lips. " I have refused it to him, you know, more than once : but now he is dying, he writes—dying in a workhouse. And he is old, just my age. Who would have thought that we two, he and I, should have lived so long ? Well, he begs me, for the love of God, and for the sake of old times, *not* to let him die in a workhouse. Must I, Bridget ?"

But Bridget, frightened at her mistress's looks, made no answer.

" I should have done it, a few years ago ; I know I should ; but now——"

She hesitated ; and then, turning to me, said, more quietly,

" I cannot judge the thing myself. Winifred, you are a good woman, you may. This man has been the curse of my life. He helped to ruin my husband—he blasted the happiness of my daughter. He was a liar, a profligate, a swindler—everything I most hated, and hate still ! Why he has been left to cumber the earth these eighty years—a blessing to no human being, and a torment to whosoever had to do with him—God knows! I have thought sometimes, were I Providence, he should have died long ago, or, better, never been born."

She spoke passionately—ay, in spite of her years and her feebleness—and her faded eyes glowed with all the indignation of youth; only hers was no personal anger, or desire of vengeance, but that righteous wrath against evil and the doers of it, which we believe to be one of the attributes of Divinity itself.

"What do you say, Winifred? Tell me—for I dare not judge the matter myself—shall I leave him where he is, to die the death of the wicked, or have pity upon him? Justice or mercy, which shall it be?"

I could not tell: I was utterly bewildered. One only thing came into my mind to say, and I said it:

"Was anybody fond of him? Was *she* fond of him?"

Oh, the look of her—dead Adrienne's mother! I shall never forget it. Agony—bitterness—

tender remembrance—the struggle to be just, but not unmerciful; in all these I could trace the faint reflection of what that terrible grief, buried so long, must once have been.

At length she said calmly,

" You are right : I see it now. Yes, I will own the truth; she was fond of him. And that decides the question."

It was decided, for Lady de Bougainville evidently could not brook much discussion of the matter. We arranged that my husband should take upon himself the whole trouble of discovering how far Mr. Summerhayes' letter was true—("He may not tell the truth even yet; he never did," she said bitterly)—and then put him into some decent lodging where he might be taken care of till he died.

" Think, Winifred," she said, reading his letter over again before she gave it to me to give to my husband,—"think what it must be to have reached the bridge and shrink in terror from crossing it; to have come to the end of life, and be afraid of dying. That is his case.

Poor soul! I ought, perhaps, even to be sorry for him; and I am."

She said no more, and I believe this was the last time—except in one or two brief business communications with Mr. Donelly—that she ever mentioned the name of Owen Summerhayes. He lived a pensioner on her charity for some weeks; then he died and was buried. That is all.

The rest of the afternoon, I remember, we spent very peacefully. Her agitation seemed to have entirely passed away, leaving her more gentle, even more cheerful than usual. She talked no more about the past, but wholly of the future—my future, and that of the little one that was coming to me. Many wise and good words she said—as from a mother to a mother—about the bringing up, for God's glory and its parents' blessing, of that best gift of Heaven, and best teacher under heaven, a little, white-souled, innocent child.

Then she insisted on walking with me to the park-gates, her first walk for many days. It had been an inclement winter, and for weeks she had been unable to cross the threshold, even to go to church. But to-day was so mild and bright that she thought she would venture.

"Only don't tell Bridget; for I can walk back quite well alone, with the help of my capital stick," without which she never walked a step now. At first she had disliked using it very much, but now she called it " her good friend."

On it she leaned, gently declining my arm, saying I was the invalid and she must rather take care of me; and so we walked together, slowly and contentedly, down the elm avenue. It was quite bare of leaves, but beautiful still: the fine tracery of the branches outlined sharp against the sky—that special loveliness of winter trees which summer never shows. She noticed this: noticed, too, with her quick eye for all these things, the first beginning of spring —a little February daisy peeping up through the grass. And then she stood and listened to a vociferous robin-redbreast, opening his mouth and singing loud, as winter robins always seem to do, from the elm-bough overhead.

"I like the robin," she said. "He is such a brave bird."

When we reached the park-gates she turned a little paler, and leant heavier on her stick. I was afraid she was very tired, and said so.

"My dear, I am always tired now." Then, patting my hand with a bright smile—nay, more than bright, actually radiant—she added, "Never mind, I shall be all right soon."

I watched her, after we had parted—just as we always parted—with a tender kiss, and a warning to "take great care of myself:" watched her, I knew not why, except that I so loved to do it, until she was out of sight, and then went satisfied home; ignorant—oh, how ignorant!—that it was my last sight of her, consciously, in this world.

That night my trouble came upon me unawares. We had a sore struggle for our lives, my baby and I. I remember nothing about her birth—poor little lamb!—nor for weeks after it. My head went wrong; and I had rather not think

any more than I can help, even now, of that
dreadful time.

During my delirium, among all the horrible
figures that filled my room, I recall one—not
horrible, but sweet—which came and stood at
my bedside, looking at me with the saddest,
tenderest eyes. I took it, they tell me, for the
Virgin Mary, of whom 1 had just read some
Catholic legend that the Mother of Christ comes
herself to fetch the souls of all women who die
in childbirth. I thought she had come for mine.
Only she was not the young Madonna, fair and
calm; she was Mary grown old, inured to many
sorrows, heart-pierced with many swords, yet
living still; Mary, mother of the Lord, human
and full of frailty, yet, like her Son, " made perfect through suffering," as, please God! we all
may be made. And when the vision departed,
they tell me I missed it, and mourned for it, and
raved for days about " my Virgin Mary;" but
she never came again.

When I woke up from my illness I was not
at home, but in a quiet lodging by the sea, with

kind though strange faces about me, and my husband constantly at my side. He had never left me, indeed, but I did not know him; I hardly did, even in my right mind. He had grown so much older, and some of his pretty curly locks —little Josephine's are just like them—had turned quite grey.

It was he who told me, cautiously and by slow degrees, how ill I had been, and how I had still, by the mercy of God, a little Josephine— a healthy, living daughter—waiting for me at home at Brierley.

"But who has taken charge of her all this while?" I asked. And gradually, as the interests and needs of life came back upon me again, I became excessively anxious and unhappy, until a new thought struck me: "Oh, her godmother; she would send for baby and take care of her. Then she would be quite safe, I know."

My husband was silent.

"Has her godmother seen her?"

"Once."

"Only once!"—a little disappointed, till I re-membered how feeble Lady de Bougainville was. "She has not got my little lamb with her, then. But she has seen her. When will she see her again—when?"

"Some day," Edward said gently, tightening his hold of my hand. "Some day, my wife. But her godmother does not want her now. She has her own children again."

And so I learnt, as tenderly as my husband could break it to me, that Lady de Bougainville had, according to the word she used of her own dear ones, "gone away;" and that when I went home to my little Josephine I should find *her* place vacant; that on this side the grave I should see the face I loved no more.

It seemed that my vision of the Virgin Mary was reality: that, hearing of my extreme dan-ger, Lady de Bougainville had risen from her bed, in the middle of the night—a wild, stormy winter's night—and come to me; had sat by me, tended me, and with her indomitable hope and courage kept from sinking into utter despair my poor husband and my father, until the trial was over, and mine and baby's life were safe. Then she went home, troubling no one, complaining to no one, and lay down on her bed to rise up no more.

She was ill a few days—only a few; and every one thought she would be better very soon, until she was actually dying. It was just about midnight, and all her faithful and attached servants hastily gathered round her, but too late. She knew no one, and said not a single word to any one, but just lay, sleeping into death, as it were, as quiet as an hour-old child. Only once, a few minutes before her departure, catching suddenly at the hand which held hers, and opening her eyes wide, she fixed them steadily upon the empty space at the foot of her bed.

" Look, Bridget !" she said in a joyful voice, " Look ! the children—the children !"

It might have been ;—God knows!

* * * * * * *

It was spring—full, bright, cheerful May— when, carrying our little daughter in his arms, my husband took me for the first time to see the new grave which had risen up beside the others in Brierley churchyard. I sat down by it; put its pretty primroses, already so numerous, into my baby's hands, and talked to her unheeding ears about her godmother.

But all the while I had no feeling whatever, and I never have had since, that it was really *herself* who lay sleeping there: she, who to the last day of her long term of years was such a brave lady; so full of energy, activity, courage, and strength—whose whole thoughts were not for herself but for others—who was for ever busy doing good. She was doing the same somewhere else, I was certain; carrying out the same heroic life, loving with the same warm heart, rejoicing with a keener and more perfect joy.

And so I think of her still; and I *will* think

of her, and I will not grieve. But I know that on earth I shall never again behold the like of my dear Lady de Bougainville.

THE END.

LONDON : PRINTED BY MACDONALD AND TUGWELL, BLENHEIM HOUSE

HURST AND BLACKETT'S

New Publications.

MESSRS. HURST AND BLACKETT'S

LIST OF NEW WORKS.

VOL. II. OF HER MAJESTY'S TOWER. By W. HEPWORTH DIXON. DEDICATED BY EXPRESS PERMISSION TO THE QUEEN. *Fifth Edition.* Demy 8vo. 15s.

CONTENTS:—The Anglo-Spanish Plot—Factions at Court—Lord Grey of Wilton—Old English Catholics—The English Jesuits—White Webbs—The Priests' Plot—Wilton Court—Last of a Noble Line—Powder-Plot Room—Guy Fawkes—Origin of the Plot—Vinegar House—Conspiracy at Large—The Jesuit's Move—In London—November, 1605—Hunted Down—In the Tower—Search for Garnet—End of the English Jesuits—The Catholic Lords—Harry Percy—The Wizard Earl—A Real Arabella Plot—William Seymour—The Escape—Pursuit—Dead in the Tower—Lady Frances Howard—Robert Carr—Powder Poisoning—The End.

FROM THE TIMES:—"All the civilized world—English, Continental, and American—takes an interest in the Tower of London. The Tower is the stage upon which has been enacted some of the grandest dramas and saddest tragedies in our national annals. If, in imagination, we take our stand on those time-worn walls, and let century after century flit past us, we shall see in due succession the majority of the most famous men and lovely women of England in the olden time. We shall see them jesting, jousting, love-making, plotting, and then anon, perhaps, commending their souls to God in the presence of a hideous masked figure, bearing an axe in his hands. It is such pictures as these that Mr. Dixon, with considerable skill as an historical limner, has set before us in these volumes. Mr. Dixon dashes off the scenes of Tower history with great spirit. His descriptions are given with such terseness and vigour that we should spoil them by any attempt at condensation. As favourable examples of his narrative powers we may call attention to the story of the beautiful but unpopular Elinor, Queen of Henry III., and the description of Anne Boleyn's first and second arrivals at the Tower. Then we have the story of the bold Bishop of Durham, who escapes by the aid of a cord hidden in a wine jar; and the tale of Maud Fitzwalter, imprisoned and murdered by the caitiff John. Passing onwards, we meet Charles of Orleans, the poetic French Prince, captured at Agincourt, and detained for five-and-twenty years a prisoner in the Tower. Next we encounter the baleful form of Richard of Gloucester, and are filled with indignation at the blackest of the black Tower deeds. As we draw nearer to modern times, we have the sorrowful story of the Nine Days' Queen, poor little Lady Jane Grey. The chapter entitled "No Cross, no Crown" is one of the most affecting in the book. A mature man can scarcely read it without feeling the tears ready to trickle from his eyes. No part of the first volume yields in interest to the chapters which are devoted to the story of Sir Walter Raleigh. The greater part of the second volume is occupied with the story of the Gunpowder Plot. The narrative is extremely interesting, and will repay perusal. Another *cause célèbre* possessed of a perennial interest, is the murder of Sir Thomas Overbury by Lord and Lady Somerset. Mr. Dixon tells the tale skilfully. In conclusion, we may congratulate the author on this, his latest work. Both volumes are decidedly attractive, and throw much light on our national history, but we think the palm of superior interest must be awarded to the second volume."

FROM THE ATHENÆUM:—"The present volume is superior in sustained interest to that by which it was preceded. The whole details are so picturesquely narrated, that the reader is carried away by the narrative. The stories are told with such knowledge of new facts as to make them like hitherto unwritten chapters in our history."

FROM THE MORNING POST:—"This volume fascinates the reader's imagination and stimulates his curiosity, whilst throwing floods of pure light on several of the most perplexing matters of James the First's reign. Not interior to any of the author's previous works of history in respect of discernment and logical soundness, it equals them in luminous expression, and surpasses some of them in romantic interest."

MESSRS. HURST AND BLACKETT'S
NEW WORKS—*Continued.*

VOL. I. OF HER MAJESTY'S TOWER. By W.
HEPWORTH DIXON. DEDICATED BY EXPRESS PERMIS-
SION TO THE QUEEN. *Sixth Edition.* Demy 8vo. 15s.

CONTENTS:—The Pile—Inner Ward and Outer Ward—The Wharf—River Rights—
The White Tower—Charles of Orleans—Uncle Gloucester—Prison Rules—Beau-
champ Tower—The good Lord Cobham—King and Cardinal—The Pilgrimage
of Grace—Madge Cheyne—Heirs to the Crown—The Nine Days' Queen—De-
throned—The Men of Kent—Courtney—No Cross no Crown—Cranmer, Lati-
mer, Ridley—White Roses—Princess Margaret—Plot and Counterplot—Mon-
sieur Charles—Bishop of Ross—Murder of Northumberland—Philip the Con-
fessor—Mass in the Tower—Sir Walter Raleigh—The Arabella Plot—Raleigh's
Walk—The Villain Waad—The Garden House—The Brick Tower.

"From first to last this volume overflows with new information and original
thought, with poetry and picture. In these fascinating pages Mr. Dixon dis-
charges alternately the functions of the historian, and the historic biographer, with
the insight, art, humour and accurate knowledge which never fail him when he
undertakes to illumine the darksome recesses of our national story."—*Morning Post*

"We earnestly recommend this remarkable volume to those in quest of amusement and instruction, at once solid and refined. It is a most eloquent and graphic
historical narrative, by a ripe scholar and an accomplished master of English dic-
tion, and a valuable commentary on the social aspect of mediæval and Tudor civil-
izat on. In Mr. Dixon's pages are related some of the most moving records of
human flesh and blood to which human ear could listen."—*Daily Telegraph.*

"It is needless to say that Mr. Dixon clothes the gray stones of the old Tower
with a new an t more living interest than most of us have felt before. It is needless to say that the stories are admirably told, for Mr. Dixon's style is full of vigour
and liveliness, and he would make a far duller subject than this tale of tragic suffering and heroism into an interesting volume. This book is as fascinating as a good
novel, yet it has all the truth of veritable history."—*Daily News.*

"It is impossible to praise too highly this most entrancing history. A better
book has seldom, and a brighter one has never, been issued to the world by any
master of the delightful art of historic illustration."—*Star.*

"We can highly recommend Mr. Dixon's work. It will enhance his reputation.
The whole is charmingly written, and there is a life, a spirit, and a reality about
the sketches of the celebrated prisoners of the Tower, which give the work the
interest of a romance. 'Her Majesty's Tower' is likely to become one of the most
popular contributions to history."—*Standard.*

"In many respects this noble volume is Mr. Dixon's masterpiece. The book is a
microcosm of our English history; and throughout it is penned with an eloquence
as remarkable for its vigorous simplicity as for its luminous picturesqueness. It
more than sustains Mr. Dixon's reputation. It enhances it."—*Sun.*

"This is a work of great value. It cannot fail to be largely popular and to maintain its author's reputation. It bears throughout the marks of careful study, keen
observation, and that power of seizing upon those points of a story that are of real
importance, which is the most precious possession of the historian. To all historic
documents, ancient and modern, Mr. Dixon has had unequalled facilities of access,
and his work will in future be the trusted and popular history of the Tower. He
has succeeded in giving a splendid panorama of English history."—*Globe.*

"This charming volume will be the most permanently popular of all Mr. Dixon's
works. Under the treatment of so practised a master of our English tongue the
story of the Tower becomes more fascinating than the daintiest of romances."—
Examiner.

2

MESSRS HURST AND BLACKETT'S
NEW WORKS—*Continued.*

A BOOK ABOUT THE CLERGY. By J. C.
JEAFFRESON, B.A., Oxon, author of " A Book about Lawyers," " A Book about Doctors," &c. *Second Edition.* 2 vols 8vo. 30s.

" This is a book of sterling excellence, in which all—laity as well as clergy—will find entertainment and instruction: a book to be bought and placed permanently in our libraries. It is written in a terse and lively style throughout, it is eminently fair and candid, and is full of interesting information on almost every topic that serves to illustrate the history of the English clergy. There are many other topics of interest treated of in Mr. Jeaffreson's beguiling volumes; but the specimens we have given will probably induce our readers to consult the book itself for further information. If, in addition to the points already indicated in this article, they wish to learn why people built such large churches in the Middle Ages, when the population was so much smaller than now; why university tutors and dignitaries are called 'dons,' and priests in olden times were called ' sirs;' if they wish to read a good account of the *rationale* of trials and executions for heresy; if they wish to know something of Church plays and 'Church ales;' if they wish to read a smashing demolition of Macaulay's famous chapter on the clergy, or an interesting account of mediæval preaching and preachers, or the origin of decorating churches, or the observance of Sunday in Saxon and Elizabethan times, or a fair *résumé* of the ' Ikon Basilike' controversy—if they wish information on any or all of these and many other subjects, they cannot do better than order 'A Book about the Clergy' without delay. Mr. Jeaffreson writes so well that it is a pleasure to read him."—*Times.*

" Honest praise may be awarded to these volumes. Mr. Jeaffreson has collected a large amount of curious information, and a rich store of facts not readily to be found elsewhere. The book will please, and it deserves to please, those who like picturesque details and pleasant gossip."—*Pall Mall Gazette.*

" In Mr. Jeaffreson's book every chapter bears marks of research, diligent investigation, and masterly views. We only hope our readers will for themselves spend on these amusing and well-written volumes the time and care they so well deserve, for turn where we will, we are sure to meet with something to arrest the attention, and gratify the taste for pleasant, lively, and instructive reading."—*Standard.*

" Composed, as history ought to be, with anecdotical illustrations and biographical incidents, Mr. Jeaffreson's 'Book about the Clergy,' in its general scope and execution, rises to the dignity of history. By an infusion of what we may call sub-history, Mr. Jeaffreson, in his work, appeals to the general reader."—*Post.*

" Mr. Jeaffreson's 'Book about the Clergy ' is a really good history. Everybody knows, or ought to know, his genial, clever, and thoroughly interesting books about Doctors and Lawyers. His 'Book about the Clergy' deserves to be placed in even a higher category. Mr. Jeaffreson has done his work so well, that he has left little room for any historian of the clergy to come after him."—*Daily Telegraph.*

" If our readers desire to learn the condition of the clergy from the days of the Lollards to those of the Puseyites, they cannot do better than read Mr. Jeaffreson's capital 'Book about the Clergy.' Mr. Jeaffreson's idea of supplying information respecting the usages and characteristics of the three learned professions in such a way as to afford both aid to the historical student and entertainment to the general reader was a happy one, and it has admirably been carried into execution."—*Athenæum.*

" A book which has many and striking merits. Mr. Jeaffreson's research has been large, the pains he has taken in collecting, as in digesting, his materials highly creditable. His book will be as readily accepted by the general public as by those who curiously observe the growth of customs and the influence of the learned professions upon the habits of society."—*Spectator.*

" This 'Book about the Clergy' will materially add to the reputation and popularity of its author. All who turn over its pages will do justice to the persevering research which has amassed the materials of which it is composed, and the admirable skill with which those materials have been classified and displayed."—*Sun.*

" A most interesting and valuable work, full of curious and amusing information."—*Globe.*

" Mr. Jeaffreson has succeeded in writing a full and exhaustive history of the English clergy. His work will interest and attract all classes of readers "—*Observer.*

MESSRS. HURST AND BLACKETT'S
NEW WORKS—*Continued.*

FRANCIS THE FIRST IN CAPTIVITY AT MADRID, AND OTHER HISTORIC STUDIES. By A. BAILLIE COCHRANE. *Second Edition.* 2 vols. post 8vo. 21s.

"A pleasant, interesting, and entertaining work."—*Daily News.*

"These eloquent volumes contain three interesting and instructive studies: Francis the First,' 'The Council of Blood,' and 'The Flight of Varennes.' It will not lessen the attraction of their bright pages that the author deals mainly with the romantic elements of these historical passages."—*Morning Post.*

"The first volume of Mr. Cochrane's new work contains a history of Francis I. from his accession to his release from his captivity in Spain. The second contains 'The Council of Blood,' a narrative of the tragic end which befel the chivalrous but too credulous Count Egmont; and, lastly, the unsuccessful attempt of the Royal Family of France to escape from Paris in 1789, known as the 'Flight of Varennes.' Each of these episodes affords scope for highly dramatic treatment, and we have to congratulate Mr. Cochrane upon a very successful attempt to bring strongly into the foreground three very momentous occurrences in the history of the last three centuries. We strongly recommend these volumes to our readers."—*Globe.*

SPIRITUAL WIVES. By W. HEPWORTH DIXON, Author of 'NEW AMERICA,' &c. FOURTH EDITION, with A NEW PREFACE. 2 vols. 8vo. With Portrait of the Author. 30s.

"Mr. Dixon has treated his subject in a philosophical spirit, and in his usual graphic manner. There is, to our thinking, more pernicious doctrine in one chapter of some of the sensational novels which find admirers in drawing-rooms and eulogists in the press than in the whole of Mr. Dixon's interesting work."—*Examiner.*

"No more wondrous narrative of human passion and romance, no stranger contribution to the literature of psychology than Mr. Dixon's book has been published since man first began to seek after the laws that govern the moral and intellectual life of the human race. To those readers who seek in current literature the pleasures of intellectual excitement we commend it as a work that affords more entertainment than can be extracted from a score of romances. But its power to amuse is less noteworthy than its instructiveness on matters of highest moment. 'Spiritual Wives' will be studied with no less profit than interest."—*Morning Post.*

THE LIFE OF ROSSINI. By H. SUTHERLAND EDWARDS. 1 vol. 8vo, with fine Portrait. 15s

"An eminently interesting, readable, and trustworthy book. Mr. Edwards was instinctively looked to for a life of Rossini, and the result is a very satisfactory one. The salient features of Rossini's life and labours are grouped in admirable order; and the book, while it conveys everything necessary to an accurate idea of its subject, is as interesting as a novel."—*Sunday Times.*

"Mr. Sutherland Edwards is thoroughly qualified to be Rossini's biographer. To a sound judgment and elegant taste, he adds a competent share of artistic and technical acquirements. In his narrative of facts he is useful and accurate; and his opinions are uniformly candid and dispassionate. His work is written with easy and unaffected grace; and we have nowhere met with a more judicious estimate of the artistic and personal character of one of the brightest luminaries of the nineteenth century."—*Illustrated News.*

"Rossini's life has been well written by Mr. Edwards. It will amuse everybody."—*Telegraph.*

THE GLADSTONE GOVERNMENT: Being CABINET PICTURES. By a TEMPLAR. 1 vol. demy 8vo. 14s.

"No small measure of commendation is due to the Templar, who writes with a skilful pen, and displays such knowledge of political men and cliques. This acceptable book is sure to be in demand, for it supplies just such information as general readers like to have about men of mark."—*Athenæum.*

"This book, which merits attention, contains an interesting account of the principal persons who figure in the present Cabinet."—*Pall Mall Gazette.*

4

MESSRS. HURST AND BLACKETT'S
NEW WORKS—*Continued.*

LIFE AND REMAINS OF ROBERT LEE, D.D.,

F.R.S.E., Minister of the Church and Parish of Old Greyfriars, Professor of Biblical Criticism and Antiquities in the University of Edinburgh, Dean of the Chapel Royal of Holyrood, and Chaplain in Ordinary to the Queen. By ROBERT HERBERT STORY, Minister of Rosneath; with an Introductory Chapter by Mrs. OLIPHANT, author of "The Life of the Rev. Edward Irving," &c. 2 vols. demy 8vo, with Portrait. 30s.

"We need make no apology to our readers for calling their attention to the life and writings of a man who, by the force and energy of his character, has left an indelible mark on the annals of his country. It is but a small thing for a man to leave a mere name behind him, even though that name be famous; it is a far higher merit to bequeath to posterity a living influence, and this Dr. Lee has certainly accomplished. We cordially commend the perusal of this book to everybody."—*Times.*

"This memoir fulfils one of the best uses of biography, in making us acquainted not only with a man of remarkable character, talent, and energy, but in throwing light upon a very distinct phase of society. It is a very curious and important chapter of contemporary history, as well as the story of a good and able life, devoted to the service of God and man. Such a book as the present is admirably fitted to supply the knowledge which is necessary to any true comprehension of the aims and reasonings of the mass of the Scotch people,—and as such we recommend it to the intelligent reader. Besides this—if we may use the expression—historical interest Mr. Story has succeeded in calling forth a very distinct individual portrait. The extracts from Dr. Lee's common-place book are full of a serious and genuine thoughtfulness: there is much reality and life in them, and nothing can surpass their good sense and unexaggerated liberality of tone."—*Spectator.*

"Mr. Story has done his work remarkably well: with clear insight into the character of the remarkable man whose career he delineates, with precision of speech and thought, with moderation, judgment, and intelligent sympathy. Mrs. Oliphant's preliminary sketch is brief, but to the point, and worthy of the authoress of 'The Life of Edward Irving,' and the inimitable 'Salem Chapel.' The selections from Dr. Lee's own writings and speeches are excellently made, and are often highly characteristic. The whole work is a faithful record of a remarkable career, drawn for the most part in the words of the man himself, and none the less valuable on that account."—*Fraser's Magazine.*

"By all to whom the recent history of the Church of Scotland has any interest, this book will be valued as a most important and instructive record; and to the personal friends of Dr. Lee it will be most welcome as a worthy memorial of his many labours, his great talents, and his public and private virtues. The character of Dr. Lee's work, and the character of the man who did it, are very clearly, fully, and firmly portrayed in Mr. Story's memoir. The tone of the book is manly and liberal."—*Scotsman.*

"This is an interesting book. Dr. Lee has been fortunate in his biographer. A more striking story of the gradual rise and thorough self-cultivation of a determined inborn student, it would be difficult to name."—*Pall Mall Gazette.*

PRINCE CHARLES AND THE SPANISH

MARRIAGE: A Chapter of English History, 1617 to 1623; from Unpublished Documents in the Archives of Simancas, Venice, and Brussels. By SAMUEL RAWSON GARDINER. 2 vols. 8vo. 30s.

"We commend Mr. Gardiner's volumes to all students of history. They have the merit of being forcibly and ably written; and they present intelligent, graphic, and reliable pictures of the period to which they relate."—*Examiner.*

"A work which has the fullest claim to fill up part of the gap in English history between the period treated by Mr. Froude and that treated by Lord Macaulay, and to take rank with the writings of these historians. The book is not merely an account of the Spanish marriage, but the best and most authentic account of that critical time of English history which preceded and led to the civil war."—*Guardian.*

MESSRS. HURST AND BLACKETT'S
NEW WORKS—*Continued.*

FAIRY FANCIES. By LIZZIE SELINA EDEN. Illustrated by the MARCHIONESS OF HASTINGS. 1 vol. 10s. 6d.

"'The Wandering Lights'—the first of the 'Fairy Fancies'—is a more beautiful production, truer to the inspiration of Nature, and more likely to be genuinely attractive to the imagination of childhood, than the famous 'Story without an End.' 'The Wandering Lights' is as beautiful, as fanciful, as rich in suggestion, but more lively, more vivid; and its lessons, addressed to the heart and to the fancy, are drawn from sources more familiar and easy of recourse to a child's mind and experience The story is a strikingly beautiful combination of poetical, natural imagery, and pure, wholesome, household life; and true poetry of human existence."—*Examiner.*

"'The Princess Ilse' is a story which is perfectly charming. It has great beauty and a real human interest."—*Athenæum.*

"This volume is exactly one of those which most profoundly touch and stir the truest Christmas feelings—of goodwill not to men alone, but to all the mysterious world of associations amid which man lives."—*Daily Telegraph.*

"The illustrations to this work are highly creditable to the Marchioness of Hastings. They are totally different in style, but exhibit a fertility of design and a facility of execution which would be no discredit to a professional artist."—*Observer.*

MY HOLIDAY IN AUSTRIA. By LIZZIE SELINA EDEN, author of "A Lady's Glimpse of the War in Bohemia." 1 vol. post 8vo, with Illustrations. 10s. 6d.

"A pleasantly-written volume."—*Pall Mall Gazette.*

"Miss Eden enjoyed her holiday, and her readers will have a share in her pleasure. Her work is easy and fluent in style, lively and pleasant in matter."—*Athenæum.*

"A frankly written and chatty account of a very pleasant holiday in the Austrian Tyrol. Besides her acute observations of the habits and manners of the people, Miss Eden's pages show signs of her appreciation of natural scenery and of the prominent objects of industry and art."—*Saturday Review.*

"Miss Eden has the art of writing travels. Her book is a good one, written always in good temper and in good English."—*Examiner.*

ELEPHANT HAUNTS: being a Sportsman's Narrative of the Search for Dr. Livingstone, with Scenes of Elephant, Buffalo, and Hippopotamus Hunting. By HENRY FAULKNER, late 17th Lancers. 1 vol. 8vo, with Illustrations. 15s.

"A very readable book. In its proportion of successes to failures, we never read a more wonderful narrative of African sport than 'Elephant Haunts.'"—*Pall Mall.*

"The most exciting book since the adventures of Gordon Cumming."—*Messenger.*

THROUGH SPAIN TO THE SAHARA. By MATILDA BETHAM-EDWARDS. Author of 'A Winter with the Swallows,' &c. 1 vol. 8vo, with Illustrations.

"Miss Edwards is an excellent traveller. She has a keen eye for the beautiful in nature and art, and in description her language has a polished and easy grace that reminds us of Eothen."—*Saturday Review.*

"Miss Edwards' sketches are lively and original, and her volume supplies pleasant reading."—*Athenæum.*

A TRIP TO THE TROPICS, AND HOME THROUGH AMERICA. By the MARQUIS OF LORNE. *Second Edition.* 1 vol. 8vo, with Illustrations. 15s.

"The best book of travels of the season."—*Pall Mall Gazette.*

"The tone of Lord Lorne's book is thoroughly healthy and vigorous, and his remarks upon men and things are well-reasoned and acute."—*Times.*

"A pleasant record of travel in the Western Islands and the United States. Lord Lorne saw a good deal of society both in the South and in the North. His tone is good, without undue partisan feeling. We can offer him our congratulations on his first essay as a traveller and an author."—*Athenæum.*

6

MESSRS. HURST AND BLACKETT'S
NEW WORKS—*Continued.*

MEMOIRS AND CORRESPONDENCE OF FIELD-MARSHAL VISCOUNT COMBERMERE, G.C.B., &c. From his Family Papers. By the Right Hon. MARY VISCOUNTESS COMBERMERE and Capt. W. W. KNOLLYS. 2 v. 8vo, with Portraits.

"Apart from the biographical and professional details, these volumes are full of sketches of persons of importance or interest who came into connection with Lord Combermere."—*Athenæum.*

HISTORIC PICTURES. By A. BAILLIE COCHRANE, 2 vols. post 8vo.

"Two entertaining volumes. They are lively reading."—*Times.*

THE HON. GRANTLEY BERKELEY'S LIFE AND RECOLLECTIONS. Vols. III. and IV. completing the Work.

"A book unrivalled in its position in the range of modern literature."—*Times.*

UNDER THE PALMS IN ALGERIA AND TUNIS. By the Hon. LEWIS WINGFIELD. 2 vols post 8vo.

"Sterling volumes, full of entertainment and reliable information."—*Post.*

IMPRESSIONS OF LIFE AT HOME AND ABROAD. By Lord EUSTACE CECIL, M.P. 1 vol. 8vo.

"Lord Eustace Cecil has selected from various journeys the points which most interested him, and has reported them in an unaffected style."—*Saturday Review.*

LIFE IN A FRENCH CHATEAU. By HUBERT E. H. JERNINGHAM, ESQ. *Second Edition.* 1 vol. 10s. 6d.

"An attractive and amusing volume."—*Morning Post.*

A WINTER WITH THE SWALLOWS IN ALGERIA. By MATILDA BETHAM EDWARDS. 8vo.

"A fresh and fascinating book, full of matter and beauty."—*Spectator.*

LADY ARABELLA STUART'S LIFE AND LETTERS: including numerous Original and Unpublished Documents. By ELIZABETH COOPER. 2 vols., with Portrait.

"This book has a real and substantial historical value."—*Saturday Review.*

MEMOIRS OF QUEEN HORTENSE, MOTHER OF NAPOLEON III. Cheaper Edition, in 1 vol. 6s.

"A biography of the beautiful and unhappy Queen, more satisfactory than any we have yet met with."—*Daily News.*

THE BEAUTIFUL IN NATURE AND ART. By MRS. ELLIS. Author of 'The Women of England,' &c. 1 vol. crown 8vo, with fine Portrait. 10s. 6d.

"With pleasure her numerous admirers will welcome a new book by the popular authoress of 'The Women of England.' A very charming volume is this new work by Mrs. Ellis. It will interest many fair readers."—*Sun.*

WILLIAM SHAKESPEARE. By CARDINAL WISEMAN. 1 vol. 8vo, 5s.

THE NEW AND POPULAR NOVELS,
PUBLISHED BY HURST & BLACKETT.

A BRAVE LADY. By the Author of "John Halifax, Gentleman," &c. 3 vols.

ST. BEDE'S. By Mrs. EILOART, Author of "The Curate's Discipline," &c. 3 vols.

STERN NECESSITY. By the Author of "No Church," "Owen: a Waif," &c. 3 vols. *(In April.)*

HAGAR. By the Author of "St. Olave's." 3 vols.

"There are certain writers among our novelists whose works afford a kind and degree of pleasure which sets them apart from others even among the popular and really gifted producers of fiction. These are the writers who touch the deeper feelings of our nature, who cause their reader to forget that he is perusing fiction, over whose pages one lingers,—the influence of whose sentiment or philosophy, fancy or experience, remains when the pages are closed. Of this number is the author of 'Hagar.' 'Hagar' is a book to be cherished in the reader's memory as a specimen of the purest and most refined order in the art of fiction. The story is full of strong human interest, and is rich in beautiful bits of description. It seizes upon the imagination as strongly as upon the feelings, and leaves no purpose of the novel unfulfilled."—*Examiner.*

"This charming tale is in every way equal to the other works by the same clever and gifted authoress, which have made her so deservedly popular."—*Messenger.*

ONE MAIDEN ONLY. By E. CAMPBELL TAINSH, author of "St. Alice," "Crowned," &c. 3 vols

"A novel of exceptional merit. The story possesses a freshness and noble impressiveness that broadly mark it out from its competitors. The character of Beata the heroine is powerfully drawn."—*Daily Telegraph.*
"A very interesting and enthralling story."—*Sun.*

DEBENHAM'S VOW. By AMELIA B. EDWARDS, author of "Barbara's History," &c. 3 vols.

"'Decidedly a clever book. The story is pure and interesting, and most of the characters are natural, while some of them are charming."—*Saturday Review.*
"This work is highly creditable to the author."—*Athenæum.*
"There is everything to amuse and interest in this book. There is a wealth of excellent and spirited delineations of persons and events, and positively new ground broken as the scene of the incidents of a novel."—*Post.*

THE DUKE'S HONOUR. By EDWARD WILBERFORCE, author of "Social Life in Munich," &c. 3 vols.

"A decidedly clever novel. The characters are drawn with skill and humour."—*Athenæum.*
"This novel has many merits. There is life in it and vigour."—*Morning Post.*

NOBLESSE OBLIGE. By SARAH TYTLER, author of "The Huguenot Family," &c. 3 vols.

"Whatever Miss Tytler publishes is worth reading. Her book is original and rich in observation. Her heroes and heroines are pure and noble studies in English life of the better sort, and we sincerely thank the author for a novel the interest of which lies in the virtue and not the wickedness of its personages."—*Pall Mall.*
"A great work---great in its aims and the manner in which these are realised. The author's style is almost perfect."—*Contemporary Review.*

FORGOTTEN BY THE WORLD. 3 vols.

"This novel is well written and readable."---*Echo.*
"The characters are remarkably well drawn."---*John Bull.*

HURST & BLACKETT'S STANDARD LIBRARY

OF CHEAP EDITIONS OF

POPULAR MODERN WORKS,

ILLUSTRATED BY MILLAIS, HOLMAN HUNT, LEECH, BIRKET FOSTER, JOHN GILBERT, TENNIEL, SANDYS, &c.

Each in a Single Volume, elegantly printed, bound, and illustrated, price 5s.

I.—SAM SLICK'S NATURE AND HUMAN NATURE.

"The first volume of Messrs. Hurst and Blackett's Standard Library of Cheap Editions forms a very good beginning to what will doubtless be a very successful undertaking. 'Nature and Human Nature' is one of the best of Sam Slick's witty and humorous productions, and is well entitled to the large circulation which it cannot fail to obtain in its present convenient and cheap shape. The volume combines with the great recommendations of a clear, bold type, and good paper, the lesser but attractive merits of being well illustrated and elegantly bound."—*Post.*

II.—JOHN HALIFAX, GENTLEMAN.

"This is a very good and a very interesting work. It is designed to trace the career from boyhood to age of a perfect man—a Christian gentleman; and it abounds in incident both well and highly wrought. Throughout it is conceived in a high spirit, and written with great ability. This cheap and handsome new edition is worthy to pass freely from hand to hand as a gift book in many households."—*Examiner.*

"The new and cheaper edition of this interesting work will doubtless meet with great success. John Halifax, the hero of this most beautiful story, is no ordinary hero, and this his history is no ordinary book. It is a full-length portrait of a true gentleman, one of nature's own nobility. It is also the history of a home, and a thoroughly English one. The work abounds in incident, and is full of graphic power and true pathos. It is a book that few will read without becoming wiser and better."—*Scotsman.*

III.—THE CRESCENT AND THE CROSS.

BY ELIOT WARBURTON.

"Independent of its value as an original narrative, and its useful and interesting information, this work is remarkable for the colouring power and play of fancy with which its descriptions are enlivened. Among its greatest and most lasting charms is its reverent and serious spirit."—*Quarterly Review.*

IV.—NATHALIE. By JULIA KAVANAGH.

"'Nathalie' is Miss Kavanagh's best imaginative effort. Its manner is gracious and attractive. Its matter is good. A sentiment, a tenderness, are commanded by her which are as individual as they are elegant."—*Athenæum.*

V.—A WOMAN'S THOUGHTS ABOUT WOMEN.

BY THE AUTHOR OF "JOHN HALIFAX, GENTLEMAN."

"A book of sound counsel. It is one of the most sensible works of its kind, well-written, true-hearted, and altogether practical. Whoever wishes to give advice to a young lady may thank the author for means of doing so."—*Examiner.*

VI.—ADAM GRAEME. By MRS. OLIPHANT.

"A story awakening genuine emotions of interest and delight by its admirable pictures of Scottish life and scenery. The author sets before us the essential attributes of Christian virtue, their deep and silent workings in the heart, and their beautiful manifestations in life, with a delicacy, power, and truth which can hardly be surpassed."—*Post.*

VII.—SAM SLICK'S WISE SAWS AND MODERN INSTANCES.

"The reputation of this book will stand as long as that of Scott's or Bulwer's Novels. Its remarkable originality and happy descriptions of American life still continue the subject of universal admiration. The new edition forms a part of Messrs. Hurst and Blackett's Cheap Standard Library, which has included some of the very best specimens of light literature that ever have been written."—*Messenger.*

VIII.—CARDINAL WISEMAN'S RECOLLECTIONS OF THE LAST FOUR POPES.

" A picturesque book on Rome and its ecclesiastical sovereigns, by an eloquent Roman Catholic. Cardinal Wiseman has treated a special subject with so much geniality, that his recollections will excite no ill-feeling in those who are most conscientiously opposed to every idea of human infallibi.ity represented in Papal domination."—*Athenæum.*

IX.—A LIFE FOR A LIFE.
BY THE AUTHOR OF " JOHN HALIFAX, GENTLEMAN."

" In 'A Life for a Life' the author is fortunate in a good subject, and has produced a work of strong effect."—*Athenæum.*

X.—THE OLD COURT SUBURB. By LEIGH HUNT.

" A delightful book, that will be welcome to all readers, and most welcome to those who have a love for the best kinds of reading."—*Examiner.*

" A more agreeable and entertaining book has not been published since Boswell produced his reminiscences of Johnson."—*Observer.*

XI.—MARGARET AND HER BRIDESMAIDS.

" We recommend all who are in search of a fascinating novel to read this work for themselves. They will find it well worth their while. There are a freshness and originality about it quite charming."—*Athenæum.*

XII.—THE OLD JUDGE. By SAM SLICK.

" The publications included in this Library have all been of good quality; many give information while they entertain, and of that class the book before us is a specimen. The manner in which the Cheap Editions forming the series is produced, deserves especial mention. The paper and print are unexceptionable; there is a steel engraving in each volume, and the outsides of them will satisfy the purchaser who likes to see books in handsome uniform."—*Examiner.*

XIII.—DARIEN. By ELIOT WARBURTON.

" This last production of the author of 'The Crescent and the Cross' has the same elements of a very wide popularity. It will please its thousands."—*Globe.*

XIV.—FAMILY ROMANCE; OR, DOMESTIC ANNALS OF THE ARISTOCRACY.
BY SIR BERNARD BURKE, ULSTER KING OF ARMS.

" It were impossible to praise too highly this most interesting book. It ought to be found on every drawing-room table."—*Standard.*

XV.—THE LAIRD OF NORLAW. By MRS. OLIPHANT.

" The 'Laird of Norlaw' fully sustains the author's high reputation."—*Sunday Times.*

XVI.—THE ENGLISHWOMAN IN ITALY.

" We can praise Mrs. Gretton's book as interesting, unexaggerated, and full of opportune instruction."—*Times.*

XVII.—NOTHING NEW.
BY THE AUTHOR OF " JOHN HALIFAX, GENTLEMAN."

" 'Nothing New' displays all those superior merits which have made 'John Halifax' one of the most popular works of the day."—*Post.*

XVIII.—FREER'S LIFE OF JEANNE D'ALBRET.

" Nothing can be more interesting than Miss Freer's story of the life of Jeanne D'Albret, and the narrative is as trustworthy as it is attractive."—*Post.*

XIX.—THE VALLEY OF A HUNDRED FIRES.
BY THE AUTHOR OF "MARGARET AND HER BRIDESMAIDS."

" If asked to classify this work, we should give it a place between 'John Halifax' and The Caxtons.'"—*Standard.*

XX.—THE ROMANCE OF THE FORUM.
BY PETER BURKE, SERGEANT AT LAW.

"A work of singular interest, which can never fail to charm. The present cheap and elegant edition includes the true story of the Colleen Bawn."—*Illustrated News.*

XXI.—ADELE. By JULIA KAVANAGH.

"'Adele' is the best work we have read by Miss Kavanagh; it is a charming story, full of delicate character-painting."—*Athenæum.*

XXII.—STUDIES FROM LIFE.
BY THE AUTHOR OF "JOHN HALIFAX, GENTLEMAN."

"These 'Studies from Life' are remarkable for graphic power and observation. The book will not diminish the reputation of the accomplished author."—*Saturday Review.*

XXIII.—GRANDMOTHER'S MONEY.

"We commend 'Grandmother's Money' to readers in search of a good novel. The characters are true to human nature, the story is interesting."—*Athenæum.*

XXIV.—A BOOK ABOUT DOCTORS.
BY J. C. JEAFFRESON.

"A delightful book."—*Athenæum.* "A book to be read and re-read; fit for the study as well as the drawing-room table and the circulating library."—*Lancet.*

XXV.—NO CHURCH.

"We advise all who have the opportunity to read this book."—*Athenæum.*

XXVI.—MISTRESS AND MAID.
BY THE AUTHOR OF "JOHN HALIFAX, GENTLEMAN."

"A good wholesome book, gracefully written, and as pleasant to read as it is instructive."—*Athenæum.* "A charming tale charmingly told."—*Standard.*

XXVII.—LOST AND SAVED. By HON. MRS. NORTON.

"'Lost and Saved' will be read with eager interest. It is a vigorous novel.'—*Times.* "A novel of rare excellence. It is Mrs. Norton's best prose work."—*Examiner.*

XXVIII.—LES MISERABLES. By VICTOR HUGO.
AUTHORISED COPYRIGHT ENGLISH TRANSLATION.

"The merits of 'Les Miserables' do not merely consist in the conception of it as a whole; it abounds, page after page, with details of unequalled beauty. In dealing with all the emotions, doubts, fears, which go to make up our common humanity, M. Victor Hugo has stamped upon every page the hall-mark of genius."—*Quarterly Review.*

XXIX.—BARBARA'S HISTORY.
BY AMELIA B. EDWARDS.

"It is not often that we light upon a novel of so much merit and interest as 'Barbara's History.' It is a work conspicuous for taste and literary culture. It is a very graceful and charming book, with a well-managed story, clearly-cut characters, and sentiments expressed with an exquisite elocution. It is a book which the world will like. This is high praise of a work of art, and so we intend it."—*Times.*

XXX.—LIFE OF THE REV. EDWARD IRVING.
BY MRS. OLIPHANT.

"A good book on a most interesting theme."—*Times.*
"A truly interesting and most affecting memoir. Irving's Life ought to have a niche in every gallery of religious biography. There are few lives that will be fuller of instruction, interest, and consolation."—*Saturday Review.*
"Mrs. Oliphant's Life of Irving supplies a long-felt desideratum. It is copious, earnest and eloquent."—*Edinburgh Review.*

HURST & BLACKETT'S STANDARD LIBRARY

(CONTINUED.)

XXXI.—ST. OLAVE'S.

"This charming novel is the work of one who possesses a great talent for writing, as well as experience and knowledge of the world. 'St. Olave's' is the work of an artist. The whole book is worth reading."—*Athenæum*.

XXXII.—SAM SLICK'S AMERICAN HUMOUR.

"Dip where you will into the lottery of fun, you are sure to draw out a prize."—*Post*.

XXXIII.—CHRISTIAN'S MISTAKE.

BY THE AUTHOR OF "JOHN HALIFAX, GENTLEMAN."

"A more charming story, to our taste, has rarely been written. The writer has hit off a circle of varied characters all true to nature, and has entangled them in a story which keeps us in suspense till its knot is happily and gracefully resolved. Even if tried by the standard of the Archbishop of York, we should expect that even he would pronounce 'Christian's Mistake' a novel without a fault."—*Times*.

XXXIV.—ALEC FORBES OF HOWGLEN.

BY GEORGE MAC DONALD, LL.D.

"No account of this story would give any idea of the profound interest that pervades the work from the first page to the last."—*Athenæum*.

XXXV.—AGNES. By MRS. OLIPHANT.

"'Agnes' is a novel superior to any of Mrs. Oliphant's former works."—*Athenæum*.
"A story whose pathetic beauty will appeal irresistibly to all readers."—*Post*.

XXXVI.—A NOBLE LIFE.

BY THE AUTHOR OF "JOHN HALIFAX, GENTLEMAN."

"This is one of those pleasant tales in which the author of 'John Halifax' speaks out of a generous heart the purest truths of life."—*Examiner*. "Few men, and no women, will read 'A Noble Life' without finding themselves the better."—*Spectator*.

XXXVII.—NEW AMERICA. By HEPWORTH DIXON.

"A very interesting book. Mr. Dixon has written thoughtfully and well."—*Times*.
"Mr. Dixon's book is the work of a keen observer. Those who would pursue all the varied phenomena of which we have attempted an outline will have reason to be grateful to the intelligent and lively guide who has given them such a sample of the inquiry. During his residence at Salt Lake City, Mr. Dixon was able to gather much valuable and interesting information respecting Mormon life and society; and the account of that singular body, the Shakers, from his observations during a visit to their chief settlement at Mount Lebanon, is one of the best parts of Mr. Dixon's work."—*Quarterly Review*.
"There are few books of the season likely to excite so much general curiosity as Mr. Dixon's very entertaining and instructive work on New America. The book is really interesting from the first page to the last, and it contains a large amount of valuable and curious information."—*Pall Mall Gazette*.
"We recommend every one who feels any interest in human nature to read Mr. Dixon's very interesting book."—*Saturday Review*.

XXXVIII.—ROBERT FALCONER.

BY GEORGE MAC DONALD, LL.D.

"'Robert Falconer' is a work brimful of life and humour and of the deepest human interest. It is a book to be returned to again and again for the deep and searching knowledge it evinces of human thoughts and feelings."—*Athenæum*.
"This story abounds in exquisite specimens of the word-painting in which Mr. Macdonald excels, charming transcripts of nature, full of light, air, and colour. It is rich also in admirable poetry of a very high order. There is no lack of humour in it. And, besides these, its artistic merits, the story has this great charm, that it can scarcely fail to exercise an ennobling and purifying influence on the reader."—*Saturday Review*.
"This book is one of intense beauty and truthfulness. It reads like an absolutely faithful history of a life. If our criticism induces our readers to open Mr. Macdonald's book they will assuredly be amply repaid in the perusal of it."—*Pall Mall Gazette*.

www.ingramcontent.com/pod-product-compliance
Lightning Source LLC
Chambersburg PA
CBHW060523030726

47498CB00004B/1059